COME BACK *to* ME

NEW YORK TIMES & USA TODAY BESTSELLING AUTHOR

CYNTHIA EDEN

A MESSAGE FROM CYNTHIA

Ready to slip over to the supernatural side? COME BACK TO ME was originally released in the "Belong to the Night" anthology (published in 2010), and, back then, the novella had the title of IN THE DARK. I've updated the sexy tale (this story contains 31,000 words), and now Sully and Sadie are ready to hunt...for love and for a killer. Thrills, chills, and paranormal romance are waiting!

CHAPTER ONE

Her dead lover stood on the other side of the bar, rubbing his hand against the back of some long-legged redhead and looking very much *alive*.

Sadie Townsend drew in a deep breath. Caught the scent of smoke. Expensive perfume. Sweat.

I went to that jerk's funeral. Cried over his grave.

A grave he didn't seem to be occupying.

She'd even taken flowers to his graveside.

The redhead laughed. Tossed back her head. The man turned, braced his hand against the wall behind her head and leaned in even closer to her.

Rage had Sadie's back teeth grinding together. She stalked across the bar, elbowing dancing men and women out of her way. Her fingers curled, and a hard fury tightened her body.

Two years. For two damn years she'd thought he was dead. While he was out there screwing redheads. Redheads who wore really trashy pink dresses.

He was bent over the woman, his mouth poised over her throat.

Sadie was going to rip the bastard apart.

The redhead laughed. A high, tipsy giggle.

Sadie growled.

Even though she was still at least ten feet away, and the music blaring from the band jumping on stage was earsplitting, Liam "Sully" Sullivan stiffened. His dark head snapped up. He spun around, and his gaze scanned the crowd. His eyes—too damn blue and bright for a dead man—locked on her. She saw his stare widen and his lips began to curve into a smile—

A smile she was going to knock off his still too-handsome face.

"*Sullivan.*" His name escaped her as a snarl.

The ghost of a smile vanished from his lips.

The redhead shifted beside him. "Uh, honey..."

Oh, no, she had *not* just called him—

He glanced back at the redhead. Touched her cheek. "Give me a minute, Sharon." The Irish whispered beneath his words, softening the vowels, hardening the consonants. Cagey bastard. Usually, he could all but make the soft rolls of his native Ireland disappear from his speech. The Irish was strong, though, when he was either pissed off or turned on. His fingers curved under the redhead's chin. "Why don't you go dance?"

And the chick meekly nodded her head. Walked away without another word.

What the hell? Had the woman never heard of a backbone before? He just blew you off, sister. Tell him to screw himself!

Sadie stalked toward him. Jabbed one finger into his chest. "Hey, asshole. Long time no see."

He grunted.

"Tell me, shouldn't you be...oh, I don't know, in a *grave* somewhere?" She'd put him in one. It would be her absolute pleasure to—

"You shouldn't be here." Weaker accent now, but the vowels were still soft. His gaze swept behind her. "You need to leave, love."

Love. Her heart took the hit, and her entire body trembled. "I'm not going anywhere." Not without one hell of an explanation. She'd *cried* over the jerk. She never cried over anything, but she'd cried for him. "If you wanted to break up with me, Sullivan, all you had to do was say so."

The sex had been great between them. Better than great. Wild. And she was the kind of woman who really, really needed wild.

They'd been teamed up on an FBI assignment. He'd been a liaison from Ireland, working secretly with her team on a hunt for a global killer. She'd never slept with another agent before—she didn't like mixing her business and her pleasure. But with Sully, she'd broken all the rules.

On their first date, they'd never even made it out of her place. She'd had him naked in less than five minutes. He'd taken her against the wall in her den and had her coming almost instantly.

That had just been the beginning.

He'd been the first human to match her stamina. Matching someone with her *unique* characteristics was exceedingly hard.

His nostrils flared as he stared down at her. "Sadie, you don't—" He broke off, and his eyes widened in surprise. "Your scent..."

"Oh, great, you've been playing dead for two years and now you want to talk about the way I *smell?*" Her claws were out now. The fury was too strong for her control. Rage and betrayal burned through her.

She'd trusted him. The night she'd learned of his death...hell, they'd been planning to meet after his last op. She'd intended to tell him the truth about herself.

She'd never before told a human lover the truth.

But Sullivan had been different—or so she'd thought.

Liam Sullivan. Sullivan to most. Sully to friends. To lovers. *To me.*

The lighting in the bar was dim, but she'd never really needed much light to see. His face was just as she'd remembered. Strong, square jaw. Dimple in his chin. Eyes like the skies over his Ireland—so amazingly blue it almost hurt to look into them. Sexy lips, high brow, chiseled cheeks. A nose that had been broken a few times because her Sully hadn't grown up easy. He'd lived on the streets of Dublin from the time he was eleven until he'd reached seventeen.

His skin looked a bit paler than before. His hair was a little longer. The black locks skimmed his broad shoulders. He wore a battered black, leather coat, a dark shirt, and loose jeans.

The guy was big—way over six feet. She had to tilt her head back a bit to stare up at him. No, to *glare* up at him. "I was told *everyone* on your team died on that last operation." She should have been on that team. But someone, somewhere, had passed on the word about her relationship with Sully and she'd been yanked at the last minute. Reassigned to some bullshit security detail.

When she'd gotten the news about the slaughter—Sadie couldn't stop the shudder that worked over her body. God, but she could still see those photos—*it had been a bloody massacre.* One look at those photos, and she'd almost fainted. *Because Sully was one of the victims.* Or so she'd thought.

Normally, Sadie wasn't the fainting type. More the kick-ass, make-'em-sorry type, and that was just what she was about to do. Make the Irish devil very sorry that he'd ever been born.

He grabbed her. His hands locked around her shoulders, and he lifted her up onto her tiptoes. "I missed you."

What? She was supposed to believe that BS line? Lying jerk—

He kissed her. His lips were firm against hers, slightly cool, and—*oh, damn.*

Her mouth opened. She gave a little moan when she felt the strong thrust of his tongue. The guy had always been one hell of a kisser. He knew just how to move his lips against hers. Knew exactly how to use his tongue. Sliding it against hers. Teasing her mouth. Tasting. Sampling. Taking.

A ball of heat in her belly had her rubbing against him. Pushing to get closer. She didn't want soft and easy, she'd never wanted that. Hard. Wild—that was the only way she'd take a man.

And Sully, curse his black soul, knew it.

His hands smoothed down her body. Locked on her ass. Squeezed. His erection pushed against her belly. Long and hard. Thick. Oh, she remembered it well.

She remembered too much.

That was the problem.

She tried to pull back, but Sully's hold didn't weaken.

Sadie twisted, putting some of her enhanced strength into play. *Oh, jeez, but the man's tongue...*

His hold tightened. It was a fierce, strong grip.

Too strong. She could feel the power in his touch. It was a power that hadn't been there before. What the hell?

His mouth lifted, just an inch. "Fuckin' missed you," he rasped, then captured her lips again.

Ice blasted through her veins. *Fuckin' missed you.* He hadn't looked like he was missing her when he'd been all over the redhead.

Bastard.

Sadie purred, a low, rumbling sound. And she bit him.

The coppery taste of blood flooded her mouth.

Sully's head jerked up. He stared down at her, and his eyes—the beautiful eyes she'd seen in her dreams for so long—flickered sickeningly from blue to black.

Oh, no. Shit. *Shit.*

Not playing anymore, she shoved against him and managed to break free of his hold. Stumbling back, she lifted her hand to her mouth and shook her head as she struggled to deny the truth that was staring her right in the face.

No, not Sully. Not him.

He licked away the drops of blood on his lips. "*A ghrá*, you do know what I like." *A ghrá*. One of his Irish endearments. One that used to make her heart leap, but now had her tensing.

Sully smiled at her, but it wasn't the boyish smile of the man she'd known.

It was a hard grin. One that showed the sharp points of his too-long canines.

Her nostrils flared. Scents assaulted her. The same smoke she'd smelled before. The alcohol.

Sully. The crisp scent of an ocean. The sweet fragrance of clovers. Ireland.

No, no, no. This was all wrong. Sully didn't smell like decay or death. He smelled the way he'd always smelled to her. So good.

But his eyes were black and his canine teeth...they were *too* long.

Sadness filled Sadie. She knew his type. Knew what drove them. So much darkness. Bloodlust. Sully *was* lost to her. His kind lived for terror and pain.

True monsters.

Sadie had never thought she'd have to do it, but it looked like she might have to kill her ex-lover.

Hell. *Could* she do it? A tremble shook her body, and, for an instant, she didn't see his face. No, she saw the pale face and shining eyes of Jasmine. Her friend smiled, and blood trickled down her neck.

Sadie blinked, and Jasmine was gone, but Sully—a new Sully, so different from the man she'd known—still stood before her.

"Somethin' you should know, Sadie." His brogue thickened, deliberately, she knew. "I didnae exactly survive that ambush..."

Her hand lifted. Traced the line of his cheek. "I know." Soft. Sad. "And I hope you understand..."

A line appeared between his brows. "Understand?"

She knew her smile was broken. Her hand dropped. *Do it. Don't think.* She reached for a nearby chair. Lifted it and shattered the wood in a blink.

"Sadie—" Sully began.

Her kind moved fast. Incredibly so. Always had. Her right hand locked around the broken chair leg. She raised her hand and prepared to plunge her makeshift weapon into his heart. "Understand that I'm not killing you—I'm killing what you've become."

His black eyes widened.

What he'd become...

A vampire.

Sadie drove her stake straight toward his heart.

I'm sorry, Sully.

CHAPTER TWO

He reacted too slowly. Sully swore, trying to twist back, but he was trapped against the wall.

The wood drove into his chest. He grabbed Sadie's wrist, holding tight as his fingers clenched around her delicate bones. And one fact became glaringly obvious.

Sadie Townsend was a hell of lot stronger than she looked. Her golden eyes were determined as she attacked, but her mouth—that sweet, beautiful red mouth—quivered.

Sully could feel his blood rushing out. Soaking his shirtfront. There were screams around them. Folks had turned at the sound of the shattering chair.

The wood was in his chest, about an inch and a half deep. But it wasn't in his heart. He'd managed to turn just enough to avoid—

"She's killing him! Oh, my God, that crazy bitch is killing him!"

He knew the voice. Katie. Karla. Something like that. He couldn't exactly remember the redhead's name. She was the one screaming, but she didn't seem to realize that the bar she was in...well, it wasn't exactly normal.

Folks there weren't going to lose any sleep over another vampire getting staked. Hell, he could see the faces of the other vamps in the bar. Smiling bastards. They were afraid to take him on, but they were sure happy to let someone else take a stab at him. Or rather, to *stake* him.

"Love, I don't want to hurt you." Truer words he'd never spoken. But Sully had already died once. He'd found the whole experience to be an utter nightmare, and he didn't plan on passing over again.

Sadie's trembling lips rose into a grimace. "Hurt. That's all vampires do. They hurt, they torture, and they kill."

Pretty accurate—for *most* vampires. "I'm not like that." The stake was digging deeper into his flesh. Not a killing wound, but it still burned, and his kind didn't do so well with blood loss.

He could see the doubt in her eyes.

Fine. His teeth clenched. *So be it.*

Sully snarled as he lunged forward. The movement shoved the stake deeper into his chest.

Sadie stumbled back and her hand finally, *finally*, fell away from the stake when she tripped over the remains of the chair and tumbled onto the floor.

He stared down at her. Beautiful Sadie. Soft locks of blond hair fell around her heart-shaped face. Her mysterious eyes glared up at him.

His hand lifted. He grabbed the end of the stake. Yanked it out. Felt the rough splash of blood.

A choked cry came from the right. For an instant, his eyes met the redhead's shocked stare.

She looked like she was going to pass out. Instead, she turned and ran away, as fast as she could.

The band kept playing.

He tossed the stake onto the table. "That hurt, Sadie."

She bared her teeth at him. Teeth that were too sharp for a human's. Why hadn't he noticed that before?

"It was supposed to hurt, jackass," she snapped back.

His head cocked. *Sadie.* He'd wanted her from the first minute he saw her. Petite. Curvy. With that come-hither smile and those fuck-me heels she liked to wear...

Most of the men in his unit had fantasized about her. There was just something about Sadie Townsend.

Something stirring. Something untamed. A fire, a passion that he'd never seen before—or since.

His gaze slid over her. She hadn't changed much. Her hair was a little shorter. Maybe she was a bit thinner. He didn't like that. His eyes narrowed as he studied her. She still had great breasts—full and high. But her hips weren't as curved, dammit. He'd sure liked her lush hips.

His stare skated back up to her face. Such a lovely face. Wide eyes. So golden. A straight, sharp little nose. High cheeks.

A beauty, no denying it.

One that had nearly taken his heart. Then, and now.

"Ah, love..." Because she had been, though he'd never told her. Sully shook his head and felt real regret as he stared down at her. "You made me lose my meal." The redhead was long gone.

Sadie's eyebrows rose. "Tough shit, vampire." In a flash, she'd bounded to her feet.

Fast. Too fast.

Just as her teeth were a bit too sharp.

His nostrils flared. Her scent surrounded him. The wild scent of a forest. The rich scent of woman.

Odd. Humans usually smelled like food to him. Blood and sex.

But Sadie—there was a heavy fragrance that clung to her. A deep scent. Heady.

His cock tightened.

He'd wanted her like mad when he was a human and being a vampire hadn't made the desire lessen. Instead, it had just made the hunger more dangerous.

"I cried for you." The words seemed ripped from her. Her hands were clenched. Her small body taut.

The heart many humans foolishly believed didn't beat inside of him began to thunder against Sully's chest. His hand lifted. The back of his fingers brushed over her cheek.

Her skin was so fucking soft.

"Sadie, soon you'll bleed for me." A dark promise. Sadie wasn't getting away from him.

Besides, the woman had tried to kill him. She owed him. Blood, sex, *everything*.

She blinked. Shook her head. Blond strands of hair bounced against her shoulder. "I'm not your prey, vamp."

Vamp. "Sully." He said his name deliberately. Just how much did Sadie know about his kind? She knew how to kill them, obviously. When he'd known her before, he'd thought she was a human, just like him. One who didn't know about the true darkness waiting behind the closed doors of the world.

She caught his wrist. Yanked his hand away from her face. "Don't touch me. You lost that privilege a long time ago."

The anger inside of Sully began to boil. "You're playin' with fire." It was the last warning he'd give her. Sully figured he'd been a pretty good sport so far. He'd let the sexy blond eat his head off with her insults. He'd even let the woman stake him. *I bled for her.*

Enough was enough. The wound in his chest was slowly closing, but his shirt was soaked with blood. He needed to drink soon, and he hadn't been kidding when he said Sadie would be giving him her blood.

In the next two minutes, he planned to have her pinned against the wall, her soft body pressed to his, while his teeth pierced her lovely throat.

He could hardly wait to taste her blood on his tongue.

"I'm not afraid of fire, asshole." Her chin notched up. Stubborn. She'd always been stubborn—and there hadn't been much that Sadie had feared.

But that had been before...

She cast a disgusted glance over his body. "And I sure as hell am not afraid of you." She spun around and took a step away from him. "See you later, vamp—"

Sully grabbed her. Whipped her back and shoved her against the wall of the bar. He leaned over her. Pushed his weight against her and trapped her against the wall—just as he'd planned. Her breath panted out. She twisted, snarled, but she didn't break free of his hold.

Sadie was strong, but *he* was stronger. "I told you, already, you made me lose my prey." His head lowered. His mouth hovered over her throat. His teeth were burning. Stretching. The already sharp canines elongated in preparation for that sweet bite. "Now, I'm going to have to take *you*." His mouth opened. His tongue swiped over her skin.

Fucking delicious. Tangy.

His cock was rock hard. His teeth were ready. Time to take a bite.

She shook against him. A small tremble. His teeth pressed right over her pounding pulse. *So close*.

But her claws—*actual, freaking claws*—dug into the bloody mess that was his chest. "Not so fast, vampire."

His head lifted. He gazed into her eyes. Eyes that were shining, no, *glowing*, with some kind of bright light. Sully's breath heaved out. "Well, well…" It looked as if he wasn't the only one who'd taken a walk in the *Other* world.

Sadie Townsend—the best lover of his life, the beautiful dream he'd held in the darkness of his heart—wasn't human.

She flashed her own sharp teeth and growled.

He smiled.

Then Sully ignored the fiery pain of her wicked claws. He moved quickly as he ducked his head and sank his teeth into the side of her throat.

CHAPTER THREE

It wasn't supposed to feel good. A vampire's bite was a degradation. An unforgivable crime against her kind. Blood was sacred. Blood was power.

No, a vampire's bite wasn't supposed to feel good, and his didn't feel good—*it felt amazing.* Sadie gasped as a hot pulse of lust and hunger shot through her. Her breasts ached. Her sex tightened.

And, humbling as all hell, she found herself arching her throat and *offering herself to him.*

If her brother had seen her, he would have roared his fury.

Thankfully, Jacob wasn't around—and Sully was.

She didn't remember taking her claws out of his chest, but her hands were now curled around the strong width of his shoulders. Holding him tight. Pulling him closer.

Sadie could feel his tongue. The press of his lips. The hard bulge of his cock.

Voices buzzed around her. Music. Scents. She ignored them and closed her eyes to the sight of the bar.

She'd been a fighter all her life. It was all she'd known. But for once, she was tempted to just be...taken.

Taken.

The word echoed in her mind and had her lashes snapping open.

Taken—the name for the vampires who were converted. Sanity reared its head with a snarl.

No, no, what was she doing? She wasn't some drugged vamp slut. She was a shifter. The strongest of the *Other*.

"No!" Husky. Not nearly loud enough. *Get a grip, girl. You know vamps don't stop with a sweet "please."*

She clenched her teeth. This was gonna hurt.

Sadie shoved him back a good two feet. His teeth raked over her throat and left a trail of pulsing fire in their wake.

"*What the hell?*" Sully swiped his hand over his mouth, wiping away her blood, and she almost slugged the jerk.

How dare he? Drinking without permission. Vamps always thought the world was their drive-in restaurant. She put her hand to her throat. *Shit, it hurt.* Another sin for Liam Sullivan. "What do I look like?" she demanded. "A buffet?"

His eyes, still the soulless black of a vampire in hunting mode, swept down her body. "Love, you know how I like to eat—"

Her nose twitched as she caught the new scent in the air. The wild fragrance of an animal. Fur. Fury.

Sadie shoved around Sully. Her eyes scanned the bar.

Business. Hell, she'd almost forgotten why she'd come into this little shithole of a vampire feeding room, er, bar in the first place. She had a case to solve. One of her kind had gone rogue. Two bodies had turned up in Miami within the last month. Nearly ripped to freaking shreds.

Her boss at the Bureau had thought that a vamp was behind the slaughter, but one look at the claw marks and Sadie had known that she was after a leopard.

After someone just like her.

Someone who was in the bar right then.

Her kind could always smell other shifters. Her too-sensitive nose was the perfect homing device. Her gaze tracked to the left. Followed the scent. Saw the man. Tall, sleekly muscled. Long, blond hair. He caught her stare, lifted a brow, and smiled.

A smile that chilled the blood in her veins.

Wonderful. Now her night was a real party. A vampire lover and a shifter-gone-bad were both in the same place. Her luck so sucked.

The jerk across the bar lifted his hand and crooked his finger at her.

Her muscles quivered. Time to give that psycho shifter an ass kicking.

"Who the fuck is he?" The rumbling demand came from Sully. The Irish was heavy in his voice again, blending perfectly with the rage.

She didn't glance Sully's way. The shifter had already caught sight of Sully. Not a very hard task. The blond's eyes were narrowed. His head cocked.

"Is he your new lover?" Sully snarled.

Not likely. She wasn't so hard up that she hooked up with psychos. Her nose twitched as the heavy odor of blood flooded her nostrils. There was so much blood in the bar. It was a scent her kind enjoyed too much.

A scent that she'd known would draw the killer.

"Stay out of my way, vamp." It was her turn to give the warning. "I'm going to—"

Too late. The shifter she'd sought spun around and pushed his way back toward the door. Oh, he thought he could run?

Not that easy.

Sadie raced after him. Three weeks' worth of tracking wasn't about to go down the drain just because she'd gotten a brief case of lust-induced insanity and she'd momentarily lost sight of her mission. No way, no day.

***

When Sadie bolted away as if level-ten demons were after her—level tens being the absolute strongest and baddest of the demon bastards who strolled the earth—Sully followed right on her heels.

He could still taste her blood on his tongue. Sweet but tangy. Absolutely delicious.

Different from a human's. He'd known that fact from the first sip. He'd gotten a staggering rush of power and a hit of stark desire from the precious liquid.

So the rumors were true.

The blood of a shifter was much, much stronger than a human's. And his Sadie...he'd bet his undead life she was a shifter.

The glowing eyes. The claws. The teeth. That sweet little purr she'd made when he'd had her against the wall and her body had gone all soft against his.

Sweet hell, he'd wanted to fuck her.

Now, she was chasing after someone else. Another man. One who smelled like some kind of wet animal.

Sully's teeth snapped together. Did she think she could just run off with that wanker? No. Not happening. That was not the way the night was going to end for Sadie.

As he chased after her, Sully realized she was *damn* fast. Leaping and running so quickly that he struggled to keep up with her. In and out of the shadows. Around the corners of buildings. Over cars. Out of alleys.

No human could run that quickly or be that agile. But then, his Sadie wasn't a human, was she?

Shifter.

How had he missed that? And what other secrets had Sadie kept from him?

Even as an angry growl built in his throat, she zipped between two parked cars and headed into the darkness of an abandoned lot. Dammit. Good thing her blood was pumping through him and giving him needed energy. He leapt over the cars. Charged into the woods at the back—

And found Sadie facing off against a crouching leopard. A right ugly beast—matted fur, yellow, spotted, and with a mouth full of razor-sharp teeth.

Fuck me.

"Get back, Sully!" Sadie called out without looking his way. "The bastard's shifted!"

Aye, he could see that for himself. But no way was he about to back off. Liam Sullivan had never run from anything before.

Well, except from her. But he'd left to protect her. Not like she'd ever buy that...

The leopard sprang forward and launched right at Sadie. They crashed onto the ground. The beast's broad head and snapping teeth went for her throat. Sadie screamed and managed to hold him off, just barely. The leopard's teeth were inches away from her delicate neck.

A neck Sully particularly liked. He shot into the fray. Grabbed the shifter around the middle and hauled back with all of his considerable vampire-enhanced strength.

The leopard let out a roar of fury. He twisted his thickly muscled body and swiped his claws at Sully even as Sully launched the bastard into the air in a hard throw.

Luckily, the big cat's claws missed Sully's body. A very near thing.

The cat crouched and bared his teeth. Before the beast could attack, Sully stepped in front of Sadie. "You want to play, do you? Well, come on. Let's play!"

Instead of springing forward, the leopard padded back. The animal paused with its body close to the ground. The cat's broad head tilted up, and his glittering eyes measured Sully as a long, pink tongue flickered out.

"Not...your...fight..." Sadie's voice was strangled.

He grunted. Like he would have walked away and left her alone.

"Don't...watch..." The last of her words ended in a growl.

Wait—what was she talking about? Don't watch what? He hauled his gaze away from the leopard, for just a moment, and glanced back at Sadie. She'd stripped off her shirt, giving him a truly splendid view of her lacy black bra and those gorgeous breasts that he'd never been able to forget. She was on her knees. Head tossed back, arms up, and—

Her bones began to snap.

Oh, for the love of—

A train hit him and knocked Sully off his feet. No, not a train. A stinking, snarling, teeth-snapping, heavy-as-hell jungle cat.

The beast's breath choked him. A foul stench. Saliva dripped onto his face, but Sully held the cat back with a white-knuckled grip around the animal's throat.

"I'm not...easy prey." Sully gathered his strength, then hurled the beast toward the line of trees.

But the cat twisted in midair and landed agilely on his feet.

Piss.

Sully rose to his feet. Brushed off his hands. Okay, time for another round. He stepped forward, just as a blur of gold and black fur streaked past him.

Snarls.

Growls.

Claws and teeth.

His mouth dropped open. Two leopards were before him. Muscled bodies moving. Tumbling across the earth. The second cat was smaller, its fur a rich gold dotted with dark circles—rosettes. The cat's long tail swished behind it—

No, not *it*. Her.

The second leopard was Sadie.

And she was fighting for her life. *Fuck me.* Like he was just going to stand on the sidelines. He dove into the battle. Sully grappled with the larger leopard. Pounded at the cat with his fists and avoided those dangerous claws as best he could.

He and Sadie would take the beast down, together, just like they'd taken down so many others.

His Sadie was a fighter. And, apparently, she was also a large, spotted cat.

The wail of sirens cut through the air.

The larger leopard's head rammed into Sully's chest and knocked him back. Then the cat leapt away from Sadie, shaking his body and swishing his tail.

The sirens screamed in the night. Tires squealed as patrol cars came to a shuddering halt nearby.

The bastard leopard disappeared into the woods. And Sadie tried to go after him.

"Sadie!" Sully called her name in a fierce demand.

Humans were around. Even now Sully could hear people rushing toward them. She couldn't be seen as a leopard. She had a job. A career with the FBI. She couldn't afford to be careless.

She glanced back at him, and her whiskers twitched.

"Change." An order.

The leopard flashed her teeth, but her ears were up, and he knew that she heard the approaching footsteps, too.

His gaze locked on her as the change began. In seconds, the fur melted away. Bones reshaped. Supple female limbs reappeared. Soon he was staring not at an animal, but at the nude form of a woman.

A woman who had been his for all too short a time.

A woman who was about to be discovered— naked—by half of the Miami PD.

Sully shrugged out of his jacket and reached for her. "Sadie..." He kissed her. A hard, deep kiss as he wrapped the jacket around her. He would set the scene. He could play this thing out—

"Freeze!" The yell came from less than ten feet away. "Put your hands up and step away from the woman."

Sully's mouth lifted. His gaze met Sadie's. A bullet wouldn't kill him, but it would make his night suck even more.

Slowly, he raised his hands, but he didn't step away from Sadie.

"I'm with the FBI," she said, her voice clear and cool. Her hands fumbled with the jacket. She managed to zip up the front. She was such a tiny thing that the heavy leather fell all the way to mid-thigh. "Agent Sadie Townsend. I've been tracking a suspected killer in the city and—"

"Christ, Townsend, save the explanations." A deeper voice—one tinged with a Chicago accent—cut through her words. "I already told them who you were."

Sully stiffened. No, no bloody way.

Talk about sucking. He turned slowly, with his hands still up and with fury boiling his blood.

Special Agent Owen Miller blinked when he saw him. "What? *Sullivan.*" Surprise, followed quickly by disgust. "You were supposed to stay on the other side of the ocean, you bas—"

"*You knew!*" Sadie stormed past Sully. A few of the cops gasped when they caught full sight of her, clad only in his jacket. The woman was sexy as hell.

Sully couldn't help it. His gaze dropped to the perfect lines of her legs.

Oh, to take a bite.

"Sadie, you don't understand!" Owen fired back at her. "Listen to me—

She punched the special agent right in the face. Swearing, he stumbled back. The uniforms around him lifted their guns and pointed them right at Sadie.

Nope. Not happening. "Stand down!" The order was Sully's. Shouted. "Owen, tell 'em to drop their weapons." Sully knew a bullet to the heart or head would kill a shifter. That scenario was not about to happen in front of him.

"D-down…" Blood dripped from Owen's nose. The agent put a hand to his probably broken nose and only looked at Sadie's exposed legs *three* times.

That was three times too many. Sully felt his teeth begin to burn—from the lure of the blood and from his growing fury. He'd wanted to rip out Owen Miller's throat for a long time. Ever since the SOB had turned his back on Sully and left him to struggle with his new life and with the guilt of ten dead men and three dead women on his soul.

Screw the hands-up crap. If the humans wanted to fire at him, he didn't care. Right then, he wanted to know just what kind of case Sadie was on and why she'd been tracking that other shifter.

Sadie's small body was tight with her own fury as she faced off with the special agent. "You let me cry for him—and you *knew?* You *knew?*"

CHAPTER FOUR

Sully stilled. Sadie had cried for him?

Owen's muddy brown eyes swept the circle of armed men and women. "We can't talk about this here, Agent Townsend. *You* know better."

A growl was her answer.

Owen swallowed. "Wh…where's the suspect?"

She jerked her thumb back toward the waiting darkness. "Long gone. The sirens alerted him. *You* gave him a chance to run."

His stare narrowed. "The perp got away from *both* of you?"

"Wasn't your typical perp," Sully noted blandly. "Something else I don't think you want us discussing here." Oh, but the smug jerk was due for a serious set down.

Soon.

Owen swore. "Spread out," he yelled to the cops.

They jumped to do his bidding. Obviously, they thought the wanker was in charge. Fools.

"Search the woods," Owen added quickly. "We're looking for—"

Oh, this should be good. Sully crossed his arms over his chest.

"A man in his late twenties," Sadie interrupted. Her voice was cool and clear. "Blond hair. Blue eyes. Six-foot-four, two hundred pounds." A pause. "He's quite possibly naked, too."

Definitely naked. The guy's torn clothes were less than a foot away. Of course, the shifter could have stashed spare jeans and a shirt somewhere close by. Shifters usually had a backup clothing plan.

"He should be considered armed and very dangerous," she continued crisply. "Approach with extreme caution."

"Hunt him." From Owen. "Now."

The cops scrambled to obey. Sadie didn't move. The wind tossed her hair.

My Sadie. She was so sexy to him. Soul as hard as nails. Skin as soft as satin.

"You've got some explaining to do." Her hands were on her hips as she continued to face off with Owen. The human cops had scattered for their search. "You should have told me. You should have—"

"I didn't know *what* you were, Agent Townsend, until about five months ago." Owen's upper lip curled. "You didn't exactly go around advertising your true self, now, did you?"

Sully didn't like the tone the man was—

"If you hadn't bugged my house, you would have never known," she fired back.

Ah, so that was how the Bureau had discovered Sadie's not-so-little secret. Interesting. Sully had long known that the Bureau had a special division, a group of agents with particular...gifts. But he hadn't realized exactly how most of the agents for that unit were recruited.

He should have known the agency would be screwing over its own people. Big Brother liked to know everything and use everyone.

"Don't get why you're so pissed," Owen muttered. "So I didn't tell you that your ex-lover had turned bloodsucker. Maybe you should be thanking me for not telling you."

Bloodsucker? Sully's teeth snapped together. "You're pushin'." It wouldn't take much more to send him over the edge.

Owen ignored him and focused on Sadie. "I figured you'd be grateful, especially after what happened to your friend Jasmine—"

Sadie swayed. Stumbled. "Stop!" Her cry was directed straight at Owen. "Don't talk about her. Not *ever*. I agreed to stay on with this unit to help—"

Instantly, Owen went from attack mode to kind-friend persona. "You *are* helping, Sadie," he murmured as his eyebrows lowered. *Fake SOB.* "Only someone with your talents could work this case. You're going to catch another killer. You'll keep the streets safe—"

"I didn't catch anyone tonight." She shook her head. Looked fragile, as she'd never looked before. "Just let the perp get away and tipped him off to the fact that another shifter is hunting him." Her hand rose and raked back her hair. "I'm going home. The guy's long gone. Tomorrow, tomorrow—I'll start tracking him again."

She turned away and didn't once glance at Sully. Her steps were slow. Steady.

Sully watched in silence. He was willing her to glance back, just once, and look at him. But soon she disappeared into the shadows and left him with the man who'd sent him off to die two years ago.

Owen began to edge back. Cautiously, moving like a snake and—

Sully's hands flashed out. He grabbed the special agent and effectively halted his exit. "Going somewhere?"

Owen's Adam's apple bobbed as he gave a frantic shake of his head.

"I didn't think so." Sully stared into the other man's lying eyes. "Who's Jasmine?"

Owen's lips thinned.

"Who. Is. Jasmine." Sully let the power of the vampire sweep through him. He knew that his voice had deepened. That his eyes had darkened to black.

But it apparently took more than a few theatrics to rattle the special agent. Owen inhaled on a rasp. "You weren't put on the extermination list, Sullivan. That's the only favor you'll be getting from me."

The extermination list. The list the Bureau kept of the *Other* who'd gone bad and needed to be eliminated. A harsh laugh broke from his lips. "Let me clue you in, Agent Miller. In the last two years, I've learned a few things. And you know that infamous list of yours? It's not worth a piss." The handful of names. The list of paranormals who'd blatantly killed.

That list barely scratched the surface of the evil out there.

He leaned in close to Owen. "And even if you'd sent your men..." His teeth came together on a snap. "They wouldn't have stopped me." Sully let his gaze drop to Owen's throat. "I'll ask once more, and then I'll stop playing it nice." He smiled. "Who is Jasmine?"

Owen began to shake. Sully knew the truth about the prick. He wasn't human, either. Not really. Owen was a charmer. A being gifted with the ability to talk to animals. Sully didn't know precisely what animal linked with Owen, but he was betting it was a rat.

His hands tightened around Owen. Sully's enhanced strength easily bruised the agent's skin, and, if Sully just applied a dash more pressure, he could break—

"V-vampire killed her. When she was a teen." Owen's words rushed out, nearly tumbling over each other. "Jasmine—she was Sadie's best friend. She died in Sadie's arms."

Well, fuck.

Sully shoved the special agent away from him.

That explained a few things. Like the way Sadie had come at him with a stake as soon as she'd realized he was a vamp.

What a damn tangled mess. Sadie wouldn't want to be around him, not knowing what he was. She'd never agree to be with him again, unless—

His lips curved.

Owen flinched.

"Tell me about the man Sadie is hunting for you." Not a man, though, he knew that. "Tell me why she's after him."

"That's confidential. Only FBI—"

Sully laughed again. He couldn't help it. "Right. Save the bullshit for someone else." Someone who didn't know the real score.

Owen's brows raised. "I'll tell you, but only if you agree to help on this one." More confident. But then, maybe the fear had been all for show. Cagey, that was Agent Miller.

Such a sly jerkoff. "Talk, then we'll deal." Making deals was the way of the world, for the living and undead.

The agent began to talk—about blood and death, bodies found in trees, and the claw marks of a monster.

And Sully began to plan.

***

He followed the woman back to her house. He'd transformed, picked up the clothes he'd hidden, and blended in easily with the humans milling on the streets. He'd passed right by two uniformed cops and they'd never given him so much as a second glance.

Humans. Not even worth his time most days, but *she* was different.

A female shifter. A leopard. Someone with his strength. His cunning.

He'd never thought to find a female like her.

So perfect.

He used the wind, knowing exactly how to manipulate the breeze to hide his scent. And he hunted.

He watched her through the windows of her house. Watched her silhouette. Her supple curves.

He'd been settling for humans, enjoying the prey's screams, when he could have had...her.

She opened the balcony doors. Let her gaze sweep over the street. Stared right past him. Leopards were so good at blending in with their surroundings.

She should know that.

Her head tilted back as she glanced toward the sky. She exposed the slender column of her throat. A sign of submission for his kind, from one lover to another.

He purred.

Oh, this was going to be fun.

CHAPTER FIVE

She'd left her balcony doors open. The better to let in the gentle breeze of the night. And him.

Her back was to the doors when she sensed him. She caught the whiff of the ocean. Heard the faintest rustle of sound. Sadie had known that he would follow her.

Just as she'd known that she wouldn't be able to kill him at that bar. She'd missed his heart, not because he'd turned at the last moment, but because she'd weakened.

Sully. She hadn't seen the monster when she'd looked at him. She'd just seen the man. And her aim had wavered.

Her head lifted, and she moved, very slowly, to face him. "Into scaling buildings these days, are you, vampire?"

He strode forward and looked so sexy and strong that an ache lodged above her heart and heat bloomed between her thighs. Sully had always had a powerful effect on her. She'd wanted him more than she'd ever desired another.

His lips curved into a smile that had her breath catching. "Ah, love, the trellis made it too easy for me."

Love. The one word sent pain stabbing through her. "Did you come for your coat?" It had been like wrapping up in his scent—in him—when she'd worn it after her shift. "It's here, just give me a—"

"Fuck the coat."

Her gaze held his.

"We both know I'm not here for the coat."

And she could almost see, in his eyes...

I'm here for you.

Her gaze dropped to his chest. To the dried blood on his shirt. "I'm sorry, Sully. I-I shouldn't have—" *Tried to kill you.* "I shouldn't have attacked you back at the bar. You just—um, caught me by surprise." *When I saw your teeth, I remembered the vamp and the way he'd laughed.* So long ago, but the nightmares would never stop for her.

Fury, instinct—they'd taken over and she'd moved without even thinking. The stake had been over his heart when she'd glanced into his eyes and seen the stare of her lover.

And she hadn't been able to kill him.

She was too weak where Sully was concerned. Always had been.

Sully stepped toward her with a long, smooth glide. "Not the first time an old friend has tried to murder me."

She blinked. "But I—"

His finger pressed against her lips. "I'm not the monster you think."

Vampires are evil. Predators. They live to kill. Live by draining their victims dry and stealing their screams. Even the devil won't let those bastards in to hell. Those had been her brother's words after they'd buried Jasmine.

"I didn't choose this life. Didn't go searching for the exchange."

Others had. Others had bartered more than just their souls for the blood-soaked promise of immortality.

His hand moved to cup her cheek. Such an oddly tender touch. "I spent the day with you, tasting heaven, then when I went on my assignment that night, I found hell."

She shivered. From his touch? His words? Sadie didn't know. Didn't care. "Sully..."

His hand stroked lower, curving over her neck. The wound from his bite had already healed. Her kind healed fast—some faster than others, depending on the beasts they carried—and the shift had only sped up the restoration. "We were ambushed," he told her, voice rasping. "A fuckin' den of vampires were waiting on us. It wasn't some kind of cult who'd been kidnapping and killing—it was vampires. My team wasn't ready to face them. There were too many."

Pain was in his words and in the memories she saw in his eyes.

"The leader, I swear, he looked like some twenty-year-old kid."

Because he'd been the Blood. Jacob had made certain she had a very thorough vampire education after Jasmine's death. The Blood were born vampires. They stopped aging in their late teens or twenties and developed a ravenous hunger for blood.

They were the most powerful. Both psychically and physically.

"He sank his teeth into me, but I fought him. Clawing. Shooting. Punching." He drew in a breath. Because, yes, vampires still breathed. Their hearts still beat. The Taken, vampires who'd been made, not born, only died for an instant, then their bodies awoke with a flood of power.

And with a desperate hunger for blood.

She wanted to touch him. To hold him. But he wasn't her Sully anymore, if he'd ever been hers.

The hand against her throat seemed slightly cool, but so strong.

"How did you..." She stopped, cleared her throat and tasted the breeze from the balcony on her tongue. "How did you change?"

His hand fell away. "Wasn't supposed to. Bastards left me for dead, like they did the rest of my team. All I can figure, I must've gotten some of his blood, the one who attacked me. I shot him to hell. Blood was everywhere."

Becoming a vampire didn't really take three exchanges like the movies said. Just one. The victim had to be nearly drained for the transformation to work, but he didn't need to take much blood from the vampire. A few drops had been known to do the trick.

Vampire blood was powerful. *Tainted*, Jacob had said.

"Why didn't you tell me?" Hell, why the whole charade? The funeral? The closed casket? She'd thought the casket had been sealed because the damage to Sully had been so severe. Sadie knew about the ravaged conditions of the other agents' bodies.

But, no, Sully hadn't been torn apart. The casket had been closed because Sully hadn't been inside it at all.

"At first, the Bureau took the choice out of my hands." Anger simmered in his voice. "They're the ones who found me and threw me in a cell for five days while they tried to decide if I was going to live or die."

The extermination list. Her heart thudded into her chest.

His smile was grim. "They decided I got to keep living, provided I agreed to do the old U.S. government a few favors."

She didn't want to ask about those favors, not then, because she knew just what sort of deeds Owen would give to a vampire.

"When I was stable, I did my part." The faint lines around his eyes tightened. "Then I settled some scores of my own. After that..." A shrug. "Well, let's just say for a time it was better for me to go back to my Ireland."

And it had been better for him to leave her. To never reach out to her. The pain knifed through her gut. "Why are you back now?"

"Because I want to be."

Okay, not exactly the "*Oh, my God, I missed you and couldn't spend another day without you so I had to come back*" response she'd been hoping to get. But, then again, the guy sure as heck hadn't bothered to look her up the moment he'd come back to town.

An image of the redhead flashed before her. No, he'd been a bit occupied with other things.

She backed away from him. "Look, I have a case that I have to work on—"

"*We've* got a case."

Uh, oh. That sinking—it was her heart. *No way.* For a moment, her eyes closed. "Come again?"

The floor squeaked as he crept forward. "Owen thinks you could use some backup on this case."

So he was gonna send the big, bad vamp to cover her ass. Her spine stiffened even as her lashes lifted and her eyes locked once more on his. "I don't need help. I could've taken the perp down tonight—"

"But you didn't." A calm statement. "And he almost got you instead."

Her nostrils flared. "I haven't worked with a partner since Owen dug into my life and blackmailed me into this unit. I don't need a—"

"You've got a partner now." His eyes were expressionless. "We worked well together before. Remember, love?"

Remembering was easy—and painful. Forgetting was the problem.

"You need someone to watch your back," Sully added. "Owen told me about the shifter out there. Hunting on your own isn't the way to handle this."

But her kind usually hunted alone.

Damn Owen.

And damn Sully for making her *feel* so much again.

He offered his hand. "Partners, Sadie?"

Oh, it grated. But she stuck out her hand. *He's not like the other vampires. He can't be.* Her fingers wrapped around his. "Partners." She couldn't help but add, "For now."

His hold tightened, and Sully pulled her forward. "Sealed with a kiss?" he asked.

She shouldn't. Obviously, kissing him would be a huge mistake. Massive. But...

She still wanted him. The wanting had never gone away. Vampire. Human. Didn't matter.

No other man had ever made her feel the way he did. No other man had ever come close to satisfying the woman or the beast that lived within her. So she was the one to lean into him. The one to open her mouth, to have her lips and tongue ready.

Mixing business and pleasure—she and Sully had done it before.

They'd do it again.

His mouth locked onto hers.

***

The bitch.

He shifted in the darkness and heard the crunch of leaves beneath his feet.

She was letting that vampire bastard touch her. Kiss her.

A snarl rumbled in his throat. She'd pay for that. Pay for allowing one of the damned to touch her.

Leopard shifters—they were blessed. Superior. Not to be touched by fucking bloodsuckers.

She'd pay, but first, he'd get the vampire. He'd killed his share of the undead before. It wouldn't be too hard. Then the woman would be his.

The thrill of the hunt flooded his veins.

CHAPTER SIX

Sadie was back in his arms, and this time, she wasn't staking him. She was warm and willing.

Oh, aye, this was what he wanted.

His hands were around her waist, fingers pressing just over the sweet curve of her arse. Her breasts were crushed against his chest. Sully could feel the soft stab of her nipples. Pretty pink nipples. Nipples that tasted like candy.

He couldn't wait to taste them again.

His mouth fed on hers. Took. Savored. It'd been too long. She'd been in his dreams for so long, and part of him was afraid *this* was a dream. That he'd awaken without Sadie, as he'd done so many times.

Couldn't go back to her as a monster. Couldn't watch the terror on her face.

But Sadie—*his* Sadie—had been hiding secrets.

Not the fearful human he'd expected. A warrior queen, a shifter. More than a match for the undead.

His hands rose—he'd come back to her fine arse later. His fingers caught the edge of the T-shirt she wore. He tore his mouth from hers as he hauled up the shirt and yanked it over her head.

"Sully..."

The husky whisper of his name had him stilling.

Her eyes were so gold. Deep, and filled with secrets. Why hadn't he noticed the secrets before?

He swallowed back the desperation that rose in his throat. He wouldn't beg her. If she didn't want his touch, he'd pull away, he'd—

She yanked up his shirt. The garment hit the floor with a faint rustle of sound.

Then she smiled, and he was lost.

"This time...don't be easy with me." Pure seduction dripped from her words. "You know what I am—I don't need soft touches and candlelight."

His body was tense. His cock so hard he ached. "What do you need?"

Her hands were on his chest. Smoothing over the muscles and sending a spike of fire to his cock. "You." She licked her lips. "Fast. Hard. Deep."

She was going to bring him to his knees.

Her fingers traced over his nipples. "Make me forget," she whispered the order. "Make me forget everything."

Forget that he was a vampire? The stark thought ran through his mind, but he didn't step away from her. Nothing would have made him leave her. His gaze dropped to her breasts. No bra. Round. Firm. Tight little nipples. His mouth watered, and he just had to get a taste.

His arms wrapped around her. He lifted her, lowering his head and lashing his tongue over her left nipple. Nipping lightly with his teeth.

Her moan filled his ears. *Even better than I remembered.* Soft flesh. Wild woman.

After one more hungry swipe of his tongue, Sully managed to lift his head. His teeth were burning. The bloodlust rising with his need.

"Get on the bed." His command was guttural.

She wanted fast and hard—oh, but he'd give it to her.

One delicate eyebrow rose, but she didn't move toward the bed. Instead, she looped her fingers in the waist of her shorts—faded, loose shorts that skimmed the tops of her silken thighs—and with a little push, she sent the material dropping to the floor.

Her feet were bare. She lifted one foot, then the other as she stepped out of the shorts. Clad now only in a pair of black bikini panties, she stared at him with hunger gleaming in her eyes.

The bed was five feet away. But if she didn't move soon, he'd take her where they stood. "Sadie..." A warning.

One she ignored.

Her hands were on his chest. Soft fingertips smoothing over him. Her scent flooded his nostrils and pushed him to the edge of his control.

Her head lowered. Her breath fanned over his skin, and her mouth closed over his right nipple.

Oh, fuck.

He shuddered and tried to ignore the bloodlust that burned ever hotter within him. He knew his eyes would be turning and darkening into the black of a hunting vamp.

For prey or for passion...that was when a vampire's eyes changed. It had been the first lesson he'd learned.

Her fingers were on his belt. Unhooking the buckle and then easing open the snap of his jeans. Sully had never been the underwear type—not living and not undead. So when Sadie pushed open his jeans, his cock sprang out, ready and standing up. The thick head strained toward her.

She took him eagerly. Her hands wrapped around him and squeezed tight and—

He grabbed her. Lifted her high and kissed her lips when they parted in surprise. Sully drank from her mouth. Fed. And let the hunger rage.

A red haze seemed to cover his eyes. It had been far too long since he'd taken his Sadie. Dreams weren't enough. Memories were too weak. He needed his woman, and he needed her *now*.

They fell onto the bed together. Mouths locked, tongues taking. With one hand, he pinned her wrists to the bed and locked them over her head. His right hand snaked down her body. Pushed between her thrashing legs and stroked the wet silk of her panties.

She moaned and arched toward him. He ripped the silk away from her flesh. Drove two fingers into her sex and felt the tight, strong clasp of her inner muscles around him. *Can't wait.*

He freed her hands. Caught the head of his arousal and guided his cock toward her creamy warmth. His mouth tore from hers. Sully gazed at her—at the wild tangle of hair, the glowing eyes, the red lips.

Fucking beautiful.

He thrust deep into her, as deep as he could go, and felt the lash of pleasure resonate through him. Tight. Wet. Hot. Perfect.

Her legs locked around him and she met him thrust for thrust. Harder. Wilder.

"More!" The demand was from her and echoed by him.

The bed squeaked beneath them. Slid an inch, two, and rammed into the wall.

He worshipped her breasts, bending low over her, licking, kissing, sensually biting.

Her fingers fisted in his hair. "Sully!"

His head rose. Her breath was ragged, so was his. His hips drove down, again and again. Her sex clenched around him with a telltale ripple of her sweet muscles.

Her climax was close, bearing down on her.

Faster, faster, he thrust into her. She smiled, then she moaned, and the tips of her claws dug into his hips.

She'd mark him.

He'd mark her.

Her body stiffened. Her face flushed with pleasure. He felt the contractions along his aroused length, the silken caresses as Sadie came beneath him. Her head tilted back and her lips parted on a hard sigh.

Her throat—tempting, vulnerable—was bared to him.

His mouth was on her neck before he even thought. Lips caressing. Tongue stroking.

Release neared for him. The promise of a fiery pleasure. A pleasure to end the cold that had haunted his days and nights for so very long.

His teeth raked over her pulse. He'd tasted her before. The wild honey of her blood.

Sully wanted to taste her again. Just a quick bite, a soft sip—

Sadie rolled him, pushing with her arms and hips so they moved in a tangle of limbs.

Blinking, he looked up. She rose above him, a goddess with eyes of gold. His cock was lodged fully inside her snug depths, and her thighs were on either side of his hips.

And her throat so far away from his mouth. *Too far.*

"No blood," she whispered the words as her hips lifted, fell. Lifted. "No...bite. L-like before. Just like—"

His hands clamped around her hips and he surged into her once more. His climax rocked through him as he seemed to explode inside of her. And she was with him. Tensing, squeezing, and calling his name as her second release shuddered through her.

His teeth snapped together. He closed his eyes as the ecstasy poured through his body.

Sex with Sadie...fucking amazing. He emptied into her. Satisfaction weighted his limbs.

She was still the best lover he'd ever had.

And the one who could hurt him the most.

She hated what he was, he knew it. But she needed him, just as he'd always needed her.

Her body curled around his, and she stretched rather like a contented cat. The rumble in her throat could have been a purr. *Why didn't I see it before? Why?* Maybe if he'd seen, maybe if she'd trusted him enough to tell him her secrets, their lives would have been different.

"This doesn't change anything," Sadie murmured the words even as she wrapped her arms around him.

He pressed a kiss to her head. "I know." But he would find a way to change things between them. One way or the other, he wasn't going to lose her again.

He planned to keep Sadie with him, forever.

***

It was the cry that woke her. A rough, choking snarl.

The cry of a leopard. Sadie's eyes flashed open. A weight was over her chest. Strong, familiar. Sully.

A roar echoed.

The leopard! He was close—*too* close.

"*Sonofabitch.*" From Sully. He jumped from the bed. Jerked on his jeans. "Bastard followed us."

Us...no, he'd followed *her*. Sadie leapt up. She pulled on her shirt. Yanked up her shorts. "Sully, stay here. Let me handle—"

He spun toward her. His eyes were dark, angry pools. "Do not finish that sentence."

She swallowed as she noticed his sharp canines. *Not a man anymore.* No matter how much she'd like to pretend otherwise.

They ran to the balcony together. Jumped to the ground below. A short drop, barely fifteen feet. Her knees didn't buckle. Neither did his. Her heart raced as adrenaline pumped through her.

The male shifter's scent was strong there. Her eyes narrowed and she saw the deep claw marks cutting into the side of her house.

She glanced toward the darkened trees alongside her home. He'd been there. Close enough to watch.

The light of dawn trickled across the sky. The growing light was fighting shadows, and, she knew, weakening Sully. Vampires could walk in the sunlight. Stoker had gotten that part right in his book, but they didn't like to be out during the day. They were weaker during the hours of the sun, almost...human. Vulnerable.

Maybe that was exactly the way the leopard wanted Sully.

Her throat dried. *Go after the weak.* It was the way of her kind. She stepped in front of Sully. He might be a vampire, but he was still *Sully.* The leopard wasn't going to get him.

Not without one hell of a fight.

CHAPTER SEVEN

They hadn't found the leopard. He'd clawed up her house. Left his stench all over the place, but the shifter had gotten away. For two days, Sadie had tried to track the killer. No luck.

But at least she hadn't found any more of the freak's sick kills in the city. Those poor women. Clawed. Bitten. Their bodies hanging from the trees...

"How long are you going to keep pretending?"

Sadie's gaze stayed locked on the darkness just beyond the window in her small FBI office. She didn't jump or gasp when she heard Sully's voice. She'd known he was behind her. She'd been alerted by his scent. The faintest whisper of his steps.

She swallowed. "Any sign of the leopard?" Sully had gone out with a team earlier that night to scout the swamps in the southwest.

"Hell, no, the bastard's good at hiding."

True.

"You didn't answer me, Sadie love." A rustle of fabric. He was coming closer.

Her shoulders straightened. He hadn't been back to her home, *to her bed*, since they'd discovered they had an unwanted guest watching them. It was good that he hadn't come back to her. Sleeping with him had been a serious mistake.

A mistake that had felt way too good.

"Look at me." A gruff order.

Drawing in a deep breath, she took a moment before she turned to face him. She had to be careful with Sully. He'd always seen so much.

He closed his hands over her shoulders. "Are you done trying to freeze me out?"

Her eyebrows rose. "Is that what I've been doing?"

His lips tightened. "Don't play with me, Sadie. When I had you in bed, you were growling my name."

And he'd been tenderly whispering hers.

"Now you tense up every time I get within five feet of you."

True. *Why did Sully have to be so sexy?* That tousled hair. Those deep, look-into-me eyes. He made her want to forget everything else but him.

She couldn't do that. Not again. Because being with him was too much of a temptation. "I have a case to work, Sullivan. I don't have time to screw around—"

"*A ghrá* , you've always had time to screw around with me." Sensual memories filled his gaze.

A surge of desire rocked through her. Ah, damn. "It was a mistake, okay? A weak-as-hell moment for me. Seeing you, after I'd thought..." Why was she even trying to explain? She didn't really understand herself. "I was weak." Better.

Her voice was stronger. "But we've got a case to work and we should keep things...professional."

Silence. His nostrils flared. Then..."Bullshit."

She blinked.

"You think I don't know how you feel about me?" The hands on her shoulders tightened. Pulled her closer toward him. "I can *smell* the fear on you."

Her hands rose and lodged against his chest. "I'm *not* afraid of you." She wasn't afraid of anything. *She* was a shifter. One of the strongest paranormals out there. The baddest of the bad. A creature who could transform and kill and—

"Bullshit," he called again. "I know about your Jasmine. All about her and the night you learned to fear vampires."

Her entire body went stone hard. Owen—that *jerk*. He should know to keep his mouth shut about her business. Her face was burning and she knew her cheeks had to be flushing dark red. "You don't know—"

"Little Jasmine...killed by a vampire."

Her claws dug into his chest as she remembered...

Long hair matted with red. A wound that wouldn't close.

Screams—desperate pleas.

And Jasmine, her lips moving as she tried to talk. But her throat had been ripped open.

She was dying. The light in her eyes fading, fading.

His laughter. Mocking. Close. "You're next."

Sully shook her hard, sending her head snapping back. "Sadie!"

The past vanished. No, no the past was right in front of her. She could see the fangs glinting at her behind his lips.

Vampire.

"Sadie." Her name was softer now, almost a caress. "It's all right. *A ghrá,* I understand."

She shook her head. "You don't know—"

His lips twisted. "I took your blood. You have to know what that means."

Her brow furrowed. He'd only taken a few sips at the bar. Hardly enough to—

"We're linked, Sadie."

Oh, no. The blood link. *Hell.*

Her brother would freak out when he learned about this. Absolutely lose his shit. *She* was about to lose hers. "No, that's not possible. You didn't take enough—"

His hands smoothed down her arms. His fingertips brushed ever so briefly around the curve of her breasts. "I *feel* you. Your anger. The fear inside. The pain. I can feel it all."

She wanted to close her eyes and block him out, but she knew there was no escape.

If Sullivan was telling her the truth and a blood link connected them, there would never be any escape for her. He'd be able to track her anywhere. Anytime. The blood link was one of the most powerful tools a vampire possessed. By drinking, the vampire became linked with prey. Sometimes the link became so strong that it was rumored the vampires could eavesdrop on thoughts and even completely control humans.

Now she was one of the linked?

Just when I thought things couldn't get worse. Sadie broke free of his hold. They were sharing this office—*thanks, Owen, I owe you for that, too*—so she couldn't tell Sully to get lost.

But she> could get the hell out of Dodge. Her hands were fisted as she headed for the door.

"Sadie."

She didn't look back.

"I know what you see when you look at me."

Her steps slowed.

"I didn't want this."

He'd said the words before, but, this time, she believed him, and she glanced over her shoulder. "What did you want?"

A sad smile twisted his lips. "You."

And she'd wanted him so much. The hunger and need were always there. She'd given in to her feelings when he'd come to her home, and she knew, if she didn't stay on her guard, that she would again.

She'd survived losing him once. It had hurt like a bitch, but she'd made it. No way was she going through that hell again. There was no future for her with Sully.

"I think you wanted any woman," she forced herself to say. "You certainly were close with the redhead."

"Survival. Nothing more. You know I need blood to live. I wasn't planning on fucking her. Should have made that clear to you from the beginning. If you want the full truth of the matter, you were the first woman I fucked since becoming a vampire."

Her chest ached. "You're lying." Bloodlust twisted with physical lust until the two were almost inseparable.

"No."

His lies hurt. "I know how vampires work. I'm supposed to believe you were able to keep control and not have sex with—"

"You were the one I wanted. It's always been you."

Tears wanted to fill her eyes. No, they didn't want to—they did. She blinked them away as she stormed for the door.

"Run, love." His words followed her. "But I'll have you again."

***

The great Sadie Townsend was running scared.

Sully probably should have been amused by that fact. There was finally something that could scare her after all.

But he wasn't amused. He was pissed off. Because *he* scared her.

She had no fucking right to fear him. Sadie should know better. He wasn't some psycho who would start slaughtering the innocent. He had fangs. He drank blood. So what? Everybody had flaws.

Sully prowled through the city streets, vaguely hearing the flow of music and the laughter echoing around him. After Sadie's glorious exit—he'd gotten a fine view of her hips swaying—he'd decided to hunt. Solo.

It was night. He was at full power. And he was more than in the mood for a fight.

Or a fuck. But since Sadie wasn't particularly acting like *she* was in the mood, he'd settle for knocking the shit out of some deserving prick. Because Sully certainly wasn't fucking anyone else. He'd been dead serious when he told her that he hadn't taken another lover since turning. She hadn't believed him. He knew bloodlust and physical desire twisted and turned together, but when he thought of fucking...

It's Sadie. I want her. She'd burned her way into his very soul. And, dammit, yes, she'd been the reason that he'd come back. He hadn't told her that, though. But...

I wanted to see her. He'd come to her town because he'd needed to catch a glimpse of her again. He'd needed to drink first, though, so he'd stopped at the vamp bar. He hadn't wanted to go to Sadie while he'd been hungry because he'd been afraid his control would be weak.

He'd thought if he drank first, he could go to her. He could...dammit, he didn't know. *Try to be normal. Pretend to be human.* Have a chance with her again?

But all of his plans had been shot to hell. And, maybe...maybe there wasn't a need for normal.

Two women and a swaying man hurried out of Sully's way when he stalked toward another club's entrance. He cast a glance up at the sign over the club. *Fire.* What the hell kind of name was that? The last joint he'd searched had been *Taboo.* Screwy names. He'd keep hunting, though because—

The scent of blood teased his nostrils. Sully stilled. The women whispered, and he felt their gazes sweep over him.

His canines pressed against his lips.

The scent's too strong. There was no feeding room in this part of town. He shouldn't be smelling this much blood here. The scent seemed to weigh down the very air around him.

His head jerked to the left. His ears—sharper than a human's, but not close to being on par with a shifter like Sadie—strained to hear.

The music drummed. High laughter rang out.

There were too many people around him. So much noise. He focused hard and tried to narrow down those sounds—

A whimper. His eyes narrowed. That whimper could have been a word. Could have been—

Help.

Sully snarled and took off running.

He knew exactly where the scent of blood would take him, and he was more than ready for this fight.

***

"Why the hell are you telling Sully my personal business?" Sadie's fisted hands came down hard on Owen's desk. "I work for you, but you don't have any right to tell my secrets."

"Not even to your lover?" His face was expressionless.

"Ex-lover," she gritted out. Not that it was any of his business. Boundaries. Owen desperately needed to learn about them.

"Hmmm...ex, huh? Weren't you together at your place *very* recently?"

She sucked in a breath. "If you've got me bugged again, I swear you'll—"

"Relax, Townsend." He smiled at her, an almost...warm smile. Weird, seeing it on a snake. "That was a pure guess."

***

Fear was in the air. A harsh smell, one that blended with the rich scent of fresh blood.

A fact of life...Most vampires liked fear. Their bodies responded instinctively to it. Many vamps that Sully knew got off on fear. They loved power, and they loved making their prey tremble.

But for Sully, fear just didn't do it for him. Whenever he caught that acidic odor, he remembered his last night as a human.

Fear. It had been the last thing he'd smelled as a human. His own wild, overwhelming fear. And it had been the first odor he'd caught on waking. Two of his men had still been alive. Barely. They'd been seconds from death. Their fear had burned him, even as the blood around him triggered new instincts.

No. He wouldn't remember that night.

He had another monster to catch. Buildings loomed around him. Tall and dark, with windows of thick glass that appeared to be black in the night.

His heart raced, his eyes narrowed, and his nose twitched. *Where are you?* The question was not for the unfortunate victim with all the blood loss, but for the—

"Help!" Not a murmur this time. A woman's scream. It had come from up ahead. He surged toward the building with a FOR SALE sign out front. No lights shone from within. His gaze swept over the structure. About seven stories. A chain had been installed across the main entrance.

Sully eyed the window on the second floor—the windowpane with the broken glass.

Broken deliberately? The better for him to catch the smell of the victim's blood? *Fuck. Is this a trap?*

Animal. Savage. The scent hit him even harder than the blood. *Shifter.*

"Oh, God, help me, somebody!" The woman's cry rang out into the night.

No one else was going to help her. Trap or no trap, he had to go in there. "Get ready, bastard, here I come."

***

"I can't keep working with him, I—" Sadie broke off, frowning. The hair on her nape was rising and a knot had twisted in her stomach.

"Sadie?" Owen squinted at her. "What is it?"

Her lips parted. "Where is Sully?" She'd left him not too long ago, but...

She whirled and dashed for the door.

"Wait!" Owen yelled after her. "I've got—"

She didn't wait.

"Stop, Sadie! Listen to me! I've got a tail on Sullivan!"

***

Scaling the building wasn't hard. He was at the second story window in less than thirty seconds. The stench of the shifter was stronger up there and so was the sweet smell of blood. Sully hurtled through the window. He shattered the remnants of the broken pane and felt the sharp sting of jagged glass cut into his arms and side.

Once inside, Sully rolled and rose in a crouch with his arms up and his fangs ready.

He saw her first. Curled in a fetal position in the corner, the woman was whimpering. Blood covered her bare limbs. Dripped onto the floor around her.

The shifter had done one hell of a number on her.

A low, taunting laugh reached out to him. "Like the look of all that blood, do you, vampire?" A man stepped from the shadows near the door. His claws were stained red. "Thought it might tempt you."

Sully lunged. In an instant, he'd jumped the span of the room and grabbed the shifter by his neck. "Bastard!"

The shifter slashed with his claws. He cut into Sully's chest and broke his hold with a fast twist.

As the blood poured down his shirtfront, Sully sucked in a sharp breath. Pain lanced through him.

"Came alone, did you?" The shifter shook his head and his green eyes glinted. "Mistake, vamp. Serious mistake."

The woman scooted even closer to the wall. Sully was aware of her furtive movements, but he didn't dare glance her way. He wasn't about to give the shifter even a moment's advantage.

"You truly think you're gonna take me in?" The shifter shook his head and laughed again. "I'm not made for a cell. My kind don't take so well to captivity."

He was a chatty prick. "Who said anything about taking you in?" Blood dripped from the cuts on Sully's body and splattered onto the floor around his feet. "Ready to die, shifter?"

The blond man snarled. His bones began to snap and crack as the transformation swept over him. Right. Like Sully was just going to stand there and wait while he shifted. Hell, no. He knew his odds were much better if he faced the man and not the beast.

Sully attacked.

CHAPTER EIGHT

"You've got a tail on him?" Sadie glared at the special agent. She shook her head. "Why the hell would you put a tail on your own man—" She broke off, huffing out a breath. *Never mind.* Sneaking and double-crossing his own agents was the way Owen worked.

"I don't trust him yet, not one hundred percent." He leveled a stare at her as he cradled his phone to his ear. "Thought it'd be best to keep an eye on him."

"Sully would have made any tail on him." The guy was good. And why, *why* was her stomach in knots? Why did she keep thinking about him? Thinking that the Irishman needed her—and that she had to get to him, fast.

It was weird. Scary.

Owen confidently told her, "He wouldn't have spotted Lance."

Lance. Hell. The fox shifter. Owen was right. No one ever spotted that tricky agent.

"Where is he?" Owen barked his demand into the phone. "What? Shit, hell, yeah, go!"

Sadie rocked forward on to the balls of her feet. The leopard within her was snarling. The woman was shaking. "Owen..."

He was already rushing toward her. "Building at the corner of Burns and Montay. Lance said he heard screams and then Sully scaled the wall and disappeared inside."

Her heart slammed into her chest. "The other leopard is there?"

"Looks like it. Lance is running in for backup, but Sully is gonna need—"

She didn't wait to hear what else Owen had to say. Sadie left him in her dust.

***

The woman wouldn't stop screaming. The leopard wouldn't stop attacking, and Sully couldn't seem to stop bleeding.

Piss.

The bastard had finished his shift and the leopard's teeth had clamped on to Sully too many times. The beast's claws had raked and pierced his flesh. The blood loss would soon slow him down, even as his hunger for fresh blood—*the injured woman smelled so good*—pushed at his control.

The leopard slammed into him. Sully managed to wrap his arms around the shifter and roll. He gathered his strength and tossed the animal against the wall. Sheetrock fell to the floor.

The door flew open. Sully turned, ready to face a new threat. A small, thin man stood in the entranceway. His brown hair was slicked back and his black eyes darted around the room.

Who the hell was—

The leopard's teeth sank into Sully's shoulder. "*Ah!*" He swiveled and drove his fist at the creature. The leopard fell back, dazed.

That's right, SOB. Vampire strength. Not something to sneer at.

"I'm here to help you, Sullivan!" The shout came from the man in the doorway. "Owen sent me!"

Sully crouched as he fully faced the leopard. "Get the woman out!" The fellow sure as hell wouldn't be any help in a fight. One punch would knock him out.

But if he could get the woman to safety and remove the distraction of her flowing blood—*aye, that would help.*

He heard the scuffle of footsteps. A woman's moan. She was bad off. She needed to get to a hospital, right away.

And the leopard needed a swift trip to hell. Time to send him there. "No more games," Sully snarled. He knew the man within the beast would understand him. "I'm going to—"

The leopard streaked past him—a blur of yellow and black—and leapt through the window.

"No!" Sully bounded after him. He was more than ready to hunt the bastard down and *finish this.* But his right leg gave way beneath him and he hit the floor, hard.

Shifters had a well-deserved reputation in the *Other* world. They were tough as nails, and it took more than a few lucky swipes to kill them. It took one *hell* of lot to bring a shifter down.

"No, n-no, l-let m-me go!" The woman. Screaming. Sobbing. Fighting the weasel-looking stranger. She was using up strength she couldn't afford to lose.

Casting one last look out the window—the leopard had already vanished—Sully promised, "I'll find you again." And they'd finish the battle they'd started.

Shaking, biting back vicious hunger and pain, he rose to his feet. The right leg was still weak, the shifter had torn into Sully's calf with his teeth, but it would hold. For now.

Blood followed his footsteps as Sully made his way across the room.

The woman was fighting wildly. Her dark eyes were huge, and her black hair flew around her as she stumbled away from the other man. "No, d-don't h-hurt—" She caught sight of Sully. A piercing shriek burst from her. "Devil!"

Maybe. Considering he was covered in blood and sporting fangs, he probably did look like the devil but... "I'm the devil who saved you, lady."

Her eyes rolled back. Sully caught her when she passed out. "Hospital," he snapped as his hands curled around her. "Now!" He fought to stay upright. He couldn't fall again. The woman came first. It was always about the victim. He'd learned that on the streets of Dublin.

As a kid, he'd seen violence firsthand. The bombings. The murders. The survivors left standing with haunted eyes.

The victims came first. Vampire or human, the rule was still the same for him.

But, damn, he sure could have used Sadie right then.

Sadie...As if just thinking her name had conjured her, he could suddenly smell her scent. Could feel the racing of his Sadie's heart. And could hear—

"Sully!"

Her voice. He could *definitely* hear her voice. His gaze rose. She ran through the doorway, and armed agents followed on her heels. He was so damn glad to see her. He could have kissed her.

Two agents dressed in black hurriedly took the woman from him.

Sadie's eyes were wide as she stared at him. "Sully." His name was a breath of sound. Her gaze raked his body. "*Sully.*"

He stiffened. He didn't want to be weak in front of her and the others. His arms snaked out. Sully caught Sadie and pulled her close.

His kiss was wild, and more than a little desperate. He could hear the drumming of her heart. The soft flow of her blood. He needed to drink.

But, even more, he needed her.

Pity he couldn't have her.

His arms dropped. "He...got away." His tongue felt thick. His teeth too sharp.

Sadie reached for his hand. Her soft fingertips brushed across his skin. "Are you...Sully, dammit, you're bleeding out. Let me help you! Let me—"

"Other guy...worse than me." True, that. The shifter had retreated because he'd been badly wounded. Maybe they'd all get lucky and find his carcass with the coming of dawn.

The agents were spreading out. Some were searching the room behind them. Some were helping to carry the woman out into the hall and toward the stairs.

"You need help." Worry filled Sadie's voice even as fear gleamed in her eyes. "What can I do?"

His gaze lasered in on Sadie's sweet throat. "Let me drink." A stark demand. A rough plea.

She knew about vampires. Knew that he couldn't afford this level of blood loss. If he didn't feed, soon, he'd weaken too much. Blood loss—one surefire way to kill a vampire.

If he didn't feed, he'd fall at her feet.

"Let me drink," he rasped.

Her breath whispered out, and she nodded.

CHAPTER NINE

Sully was in trouble, and Sadie was afraid. So afraid that her knees shook and her hands were sweating and she felt like her heart was going to burst from her chest.

I can't lose him again.

He had so many wounds. His chest. His arms. His shoulders. Even his legs. The shifter had savaged him.

"Don't die on me." She gave the order as she kicked in the door to her left. They were far away from the rest of the team. They'd managed to sneak up to a higher floor while the other agents fanned out below. Sully needed safety, but she didn't have time to get him back to her place. He needed to feed. Now.

"Too late, love." A ghost of a smile feathered his lips and the ache in his tone made her hands clench. "I died two years ago."

Her jaw locked. "Do it, Sully. Go ahead, just—"

Drink from me.

He couldn't afford to be so weak. Sully had his share of enemies, she knew that. All vampires had enemies. There were too many folks, both human and *Other*, running around out there with a Van Helsing complex. She'd been one of them.

No longer. She didn't care that he was a vamp. He was hers, and she hated to see him like this.

When she found that psycho leopard, Sadie was going to kill that shifter.

She wrapped her arms around Sully and felt the wet touch of his blood.

His wounds weren't closing.

There wasn't any time to spare.

"Sadie..." In his voice, she could hear hunger. Need. Fear?

She shut her eyes. She'd been taught vampire feeding was a degradation. The worst insult to her kind. The hunter, becoming prey.

Screw that. Sully needed her. Pride could take a hike.

Tilting back her head, she offered her throat and waited.

She expected the hot flash of pain that came from his teeth. At the bar, the sting of his bite had been brief. Then there had been such unexpected pleasure.

Yes, she expected the sharp press of his teeth.

Instead, she felt the soft brush of his lips and the wet slide of his tongue on her flesh.

Her mouth parted on a sigh. Her breasts tightened against him, and desire burned through her body.

Sadie's hands rose and tunneled into the thick strands of his hair. "Sully."

Her Sully.

His teeth pierced her flesh. A split second of sharp pain and then—

Pleasure. A fast, hard rush of sensual energy heated her blood. Her thighs shifted as she strained to get closer to him.

His mouth moved carefully on her. Lips. Tongue. Teeth. And it felt so *good*. As if she'd climax, with just the press of his teeth into her.

Her hands tightened in his hair as she forced him closer.

Her panties were getting wet. She wanted him inside of her. She wanted him fucking her and drinking from her at the same time.

No one had ever told her that a vampire's bite could be so amazing. Pain. Fear. That's all the whispers said the bite would bring.

But what about the rush of pleasure? The wild heat of hunger and lust? She rubbed against him. Her breasts ached. Her body yearned.

More. She wanted—

Sully.

His hands slipped between them. Caught her breasts, stroked and teased through the thin blouse she wore. His thumbs raked over her nipples and a growl burst from her lips.

And still he drank from her.

Every nerve in her body seemed electrified. Her skin felt too sensitive. Her lust too fierce. The beast snarled inside of her, demanding release. A release the woman wanted just as badly.

But part of her was afraid. Sully was hurt so badly. She didn't want to injure him. Didn't want to make it worse. So she held back her hunger. And let him take.

Mouth.

Tongue.

Teeth.

And his hands—cradling her flesh. Tugging her nipples. Feeding the sensual need she felt. Those long, strong fingers knew just how to touch her. Whimpers slipped from her lips. Hungry moans.

Her hands dropped to his shoulders. Curled tight. Held on for the ride.

Still he drank.

An explosion of lights appeared behind her closed lids. Her sex throbbed. Her knees shook.

Sadie licked her lips and swore that she tasted him. He hadn't kissed her, but he was all around her. She could feel him. Inside.

In her heart.

Her spirit.

Everywhere.

The blood link. She knew it was getting stronger. The more he took, the deeper the bond would become.

Forever.

His teeth withdrew. A wet swipe of his tongue slid over her throat.

Her eyes slowly opened even as he feathered a tender kiss on her neck. Right over the mark he'd left.

Soon, she'd be marking *him*.

Sully's head lifted, and when his eyes met hers, there was no blue in his gaze. Only darkness. His black eyes narrowed. "You know...what happens now."

No, she honestly didn't have a clue. She wanted him. Naked. But the guy was injured and, even with her blood, it would take hours for him to heal completely.

Already, though, his voice was stronger. And the wounds were starting to close—she could tell by the smaller scratches on his face. They were shrinking before her eyes. The relief sweeping through her body made Sadie almost dizzy.

Losing him again was not an option.

Oh, shit.

Realization had her eyes widening.

She still loved the Irish bastard.

"We need...to get out of here," he said.

A nod. That was all she could manage at the moment.

"Your blood—it's damn strong, but I'm goin' to crash soon. To heal, I'll have to sleep."

Another nod. Her blood would give him the strength to get past the other officers and to make it back to her place. Then she'd keep him safe while he slept.

His fingers caught her chin. "When I wake, I'll have you." A dark promise.

She smiled. "No, Sully, when you wake..." She paused just long enough to have his brows lowering before she concluded, "I'll have *you*."

***

Vampires dreamed. Some folks thought they didn't, but, then again, some folks also thought his kind didn't have souls. Vamps had souls. Some were just blacker than the night they loved so much. Evil was a choice, not a punishment for his kind.

Free will. Everyone—even monsters had it.

Just as creatures like him, well, they had dreams.

But sometimes, those dreams weren't fantasies. They were memories. The vampire's. His prey. Shared visions given by the blood.

When Sully slept, the visions came to him. He saw a girl, smiling, with long, black hair around her shoulders. She was laughing and pointing.

Beside her, he saw his Sadie. Younger. With eyes not so hard and with a curving mouth.

Innocence.

Youth.

A beautiful dream. Happy.

At first.

The lush woods around the girls grew darker. Laughter reached his ears. Cold. Insidious. And he wanted to wake up. But he couldn't. The sleep was too deep.

The vampire attacked the dark-haired girl. Jasmine.

"Change, Sadie, change! Help me!" Jasmine begged.

The snap of bones. The rolling cry of the leopard.

The vampire had a tight lock on little Jasmine. Blood dripped down her neck and her cries grew weaker.

Sadie attacked. Biting. Clawing. Fighting as fiercely as she could. But her leopard wasn't fully grown. The leopard aged as the girl did. Still young. Still weak.

The vampire dropped Jasmine onto the ground. Her eyes were wide open and terrified.

The vampire was going after Sadie. "You'll taste so good."

Another roar filled the forest. Shook the earth.

Not from Sadie. From another. Coming closer.

The vampire glanced over his shoulder.

Too late.

Blood covered the ground.

And Jasmine—her eyes closed.

CHAPTER TEN

Sully's body stiffened against her. Sadie frowned and kept stroking his chest. He'd been out for hours and hours. The sun was setting.

His night was coming.

The wounds on his body had healed. Not even a scratch marred his body.

She leaned over him. Her gaze lingered on the shadows cast by his lashes. He was almost beautiful in sleep. Far too attractive. No man should be so sexy.

Her hand lifted. Traced the curve of his lips.

He woke instantly. His eyelids flew open and his hand snapped around her wrist in a steely grip. "Who was the other leopard?" A hard, rumbling demand.

Sadie blinked. "What?" Was he talking about the perp who'd attacked him? Unfortunately, the team still hadn't tracked him, but she knew they would. It was only a matter of time, especially once she joined the hunt.

"In the woods that day..." Sully added roughly. "Who was he?"

Chill bumps rose on her arms.

"Who killed the vampire? Who killed the fucker who attacked you and Jasmine?"

Her gaze held his as her breath rushed out. "The link's that strong, huh?" The blood link was one of the few real mysteries still in existence. Just how strong, how deep, it went really depended on the vampire and his victim.

She swallowed. "My brother Jacob." Thank God he'd decided to come looking for her and Jasmine. If he hadn't, she would have died that night, too. Because their attacker…"He'd been watching us. For days." Hiding his scent—the tricky bastard. "Waiting for that one moment when we were vulnerable." They'd been having so much fun. Running. Laughing. Enjoying the wild woods.

His lips thinned. "How can…" He stopped, jaw clenching.

"Sully?"

His gaze was stark and his brogue thick as he asked, "How can you let me touch you, knowin' what he did?"

"Because you *aren't* him." Sully had fought fiercely to save the human woman in that building. He wouldn't attack innocents. Not his style. Never had been. Never would be.

She was an idiot for ever thinking otherwise.

"Let go of my hand," she told him quietly.

The body beneath hers—*delicious male power*—tautened even more.

But he let her go.

"I shouldn't have—" He shook his head. "That first night, I-I needed the blood, but I should never have taken—"

She snorted. Probably not her sexiest moment. "Please, vampire. If I'd truly wanted to get free of your hold in that place, it would have been too easy to do." The stark truth was that she'd wanted to be in his arms again. Her fingers brushed down his cheek. "I'm touching you," she told him clearly, "because I want to."

Sully's nostrils flared.

"Because I have to." Softer.

She kissed him. An open-mouthed, I'm-starving-for-you kiss. Lips. Tongues. Heat. Sadie felt the surprise ripple through him.

Crazy vamp. Didn't he remember what she'd told him?

It was her turn to have *him*.

She nipped his lower lip. Vampires weren't the only ones who liked to bite. Sully should have remembered that about her.

She smiled at him, then caught the bottom of her T-shirt and jerked it over her head. It hit the floor after she threw it, but Sadie didn't care.

No bra. She'd stripped down to just her shirt and panties after she'd gotten him in bed. And she'd stripped him completely.

His eyes were on her breasts. The blue began to darken.

She caught his hands. Brought them to cup her breasts. Enjoyed the strong weight of his hands over her. He knew just how to stroke her nipples. Just how to play and torment.

But then, so did she.

Sadie's fingers trailed down his chest. Over the nubs of his nipples. Sully was so sensitive.

Always had been. And when she put her tongue on him—

Leaning forward, her tongue swiped over his left nipple.

Sully hissed out a breath and nearly came off the bed.

"Ah, not the way we play tonight." She pushed him back, deliberately injecting extra strength into the move. "Tonight, it's my game." And she intended to enjoy herself fully.

Rising onto her knees, she shoved the sheets out of her way. Sully was aroused. The hard length of his cock rose toward her, long and thick.

The cat inside her purred. Time to get wild. Her lover had healed. No need to go easy on him.

Her nails scored the flesh of his stomach. Not deep enough to cut the skin, certainly not enough to hurt. Just enough to have him sucking in a sharp breath and to have his blue eyes turning completely black. Fear didn't shoot through her at the sight of his dark eyes and his sharpening fangs.

This was Sully.

"No pretending this time?" Sully grated the words.

Her fingers wrapped around his aroused cock. Stroked. Squeezed. She knew what he meant with his question, and part of her felt a flash of shame. *No pretending he wasn't a vampire. No turning away from his bite and trying to act as if he was still human.* "No pretending," she agreed, her voice a whisper. The present was all that mattered.

Not the past—there was no way to go back.

And not the future—because, really, what future could they have? She'd age and slip away one day, while he stayed forever young. No past. No future. But they could sure enjoy the present.

Her fingers tightened around him.

Then she lowered her head.

"Sadie!"

Her lips feathered over his aroused length. Soft as silk, but so hard and strong. Her tongue snaked out, licked the head of his dick, and then she took him in her mouth.

"Fuck! Sadie!"

She knew what he liked, oh, yes, she knew. Licking. Sucking. Swirling her tongue over his thick cock.

His hands clamped over her hips. She felt him rip away her panties. Then he touched her. Slid his long fingers between her thighs and pressed against her sex.

Pushed against her sensitive core, found her wet and ready.

He knew what she liked, too. He'd levered his upper body up to touch her better. One finger drove inside of her.

Yes.

She looked up at him. Gazed into his dark eyes.

A second finger thrust into her.

Her sex tightened.

Not wild enough, not yet.

Sadie gave him one long, last lick, from root to tip. She kissed away the moisture on the head of his cock. Wanted more.

"In...side." A rough demand from Sully. "Put me..."

His fingers felt fantastic in her sex, but she wanted his cock in her—just as badly as he wanted to be there.

Sully's thumb stroked her clit, making her even hotter, even wetter for him.

His fingers withdrew, thrust, withdrew—

Sadie moaned, then moved, fast. She pinned his hands to the mattress. Shifted her hips so that his dick brushed against her open core. Her breath panted out. She would never get enough of Sully.

Sadie arched her hips, then drove down onto him, taking that wonderful, long length deep inside.

They both gasped.

So full. Her sex felt stretched. So tight.

Her knees dug into the mattress as she flexed. "Ready?" she whispered.

His hungry growl was her answer.

Sadie started moving. Rising, falling. Faster and faster. Her breath left her in hard pants, her heart hammered in her chest, and sweat slickened her skin. And she kept riding him. His thighs were like steel beneath her. His cock her perfect fantasy.

Again, again, *again.*

His lips were parted. His long and sharp canines gleamed.

His gaze was on her throat.

Sadie rose, fell. She tightened her grip on his wrists. Release bore down on her. Just a few seconds away—

Her cry filled the room. Her sex clenched around him as ripples of pleasure rolled through her body. But she didn't stop moving. Rising, falling. No, she didn't stop—

Because Sadie was just getting started.

***

She was so fucking beautiful. Sully stared up at Sadie, at her gorgeous eyes and red lips, and his cock swelled even more within her slick depths.

Oh, damn. Her climax was milking him. Squeezing him so tightly in her warm, wet sex.

But he didn't want to come yet. Not yet.

She let go of his hands. Smiled at him—the smile that always made his mouth go dry and his cock twitch.

"I want a bite," she said, her voice husky. Pure temptation.

He almost came. His heels dug into her sheets. He wasn't going to last much longer. She was so hot and snug around him.

Sadie bent over him, and her nipples pressed into his chest. Beautiful nipples. He loved her breasts. Loved having them in his mouth. Sucking them until her face flushed and the scent of her arousal filled his nostrils.

His hands caught her hips as he urged her closer. His fingers locked on the round curves of her arse. *Beautiful arse.* Now he'd like to bite—

Her lips brushed the curve of his neck. She kissed him, mouth open. Then his Sadie bit him, and Sully's control vanished with a roar.

He came, exploding deep within her body. The release was savage. So strong his whole body shook and so good—oh, *fuck,* so good.

Sadie.

She kept riding him as he came. Kept lifting her hips and sliding her sex over him. The release wiped him out. Hollowed him. Made him crave more.

He shuddered and wanted her blood.

Wanted *his turn to* bite.

How did I walk away from this? From her? The questions flashed through his mind. How the hell had he been strong enough to leave her before?

She raised her head. Licked her plump lips and—he kissed her. And started thrusting again. Her sex was swollen and still so wonderfully wet. He moved slowly at first as his cock began to grow within her.

Then the thrusts became stronger. The kiss harder.

She pulled her mouth from his. Pushed up on her knees. Sadie looked down, and he followed her gaze. The head of his cock was inside of her. The hottest, freaking most sensual sight on earth.

She took all of him inside.

Sully pressed his lips together. *A bite, just one—*

She was too far away from him. Fully on her knees. He pushed up and managed to shove even deeper into her. The pleasure on her face made him crazy.

Bloodlust rose, so hot and powerful that he started to turn away from her.

"No!"

Her nails—no, too sharp for mere nails—dug into his shoulders. His gaze flew back to her face. He watched, stunned, as she angled her throat toward him. "Your turn."

His arms clamped around her. Sully's right hand pulled back her hair as his left stroked her throat.

And his cock was still deep in her core.

Her knees were on either side of his hips. They stared at each other. Black eyes to gold. Her sex rippled around him. A silken glide that had him groaning. Her pulse raced, he could hear the drumming and could feel the soft whoosh of her blood.

He would take it, as he took her.

Sully pierced her throat. Tasted the wild flavor of her blood.

Her inner muscles clamped greedily around him. Squeezing. Tightening.

He drank.

They climaxed. An explosion of sensation that rocked between them both. Waves of fiery pleasure that consumed everything. Sully could feel Sadie, inside, out, her mind, spirit...

All of her.

In that one, blinding instant, when the world disappeared in a veil of red, she was completely his. And he was hers.

His teeth withdrew.

Sully pressed a kiss to her throat.

His. Now they were both marked. Beyond flesh.

How the hell did I let her go before? The question rose again, and he knew that there would be no escape for Sadie this time.

Beyond flesh.

CHAPTER ELEVEN

Staying in bed and having pillow talk wasn't really an option for them.

Sex with Sully had been necessary, as vital as breathing for Sadie. She'd had to feel him within her. She'd needed that reassurance. Needed to make absolutely certain that Sully was all right—*alive,* or, at least still undead.

But they had a killer to catch. As much as she would have liked to stay in the bed with him all night, a job waited. Sadie's life wasn't an easy one. Not a lot of downtime for a leopard shifter who spent her nights tracking killers.

There was a dangerous predator on the streets. She had to hunt, no, *they* had to hunt. So less than an hour later, she and Sully were scouring the streets of Miami. Her nostrils twitched as she fought to catch the scent of the other leopard. But she didn't detect the deep, musky odor. Just caught the smell of cigarettes, car exhaust, whiskey, and too-expensive perfume.

"Anything?" Sully asked.

Sadie shook her head. "Not yet." But she'd find him. Her gut told her that the leopard hadn't turned tail and fled the city. Not his style.

He'd needed to heal, just as Sully had, and when his strength was back—*could already be back*—he'd hunt again. She wasn't in the mood to find any more savaged human women. Women whose bodies had been tossed into trees and left for their blood to drip onto the ground.

In the wild, leopards often stashed their prey in trees to keep other predators, like lions, from taking their precious food. The better to savor the meal. But this was Miami, not the wild, and the leopard was leaving his kills in the trees for one reason...to make the humans afraid. To leave them a message.

There's something in the dark you need to fear.

Yet despite his taunting warning, the streets were packed this night.

More prey, just waiting.

"They don't believe what they see," Sadie murmured as Sully came to a stop behind her. "They won't know what's coming for them until it's too late." A human would be no match for a full-grown, male leopard shifter. The leopards were so strong.

"We're going to find him." Sully sounded certain. "The bastard can't hide forever."

But he could kill again, before they found him. He could—

The phone on her hip vibrated. Sadie had the phone at her ear in two seconds time. "Owen?" She knew he'd be the only one to contact her now.

"Brently and Moore Street." The special agent's voice was thick with excitement. "Abandoned house. Got a phone tip—some guy swears he saw a jungle cat crawling into the house."

No, it couldn't be this easy...could it?

"He wants animal control," Owen continued, "but he's getting us."

Sadie turned her head so that her gaze could meet Sully's. "On our way." The FBI team wouldn't go in without her. Owen understood what he was facing. She ended the call. Raised her brows. "Our hunt just got a whole a lot easier." *Maybe*. The leopard should have been too skilled at camouflage to be seen, but perhaps he'd been so badly hurt that he couldn't properly cover himself.

Perhaps.

"Keep your guard up," she warned him.

Leopards loved to lure their prey in close— close enough to kill.

***

"Lance says the leopard's smell is all over the house." Owen stood behind an unmarked police car. His gaze raked over the small house across the street. Boarded windows. Slumping roof. Overgrown yard.

Sadie's nostrils flared. "He's right." Her hands clenched into fists. The scent of the leopard was everywhere. So heavy. Too heavy?

She could just make out claw marks along the top of the old porch. They were embedded deep into the faded white wood that clung to the front of the house. "I'm going in—"

"*We* are," Sully corrected softly.

She gave a tight nod and told Owen, "Keep everyone else back. We need to make sure there aren't any surprises waiting for us."

"Then, Agent Townsend..." Owen lifted his hand, palm up, and motioned toward the waiting house. "This show is yours."

Sure, he was turning things over to her now. A charmer knew better than to tangle with the killer that waited.

Sadie and Sully went in fast. Guns up and ready. She didn't shift, couldn't, with so many people around. So, this time, she was going to use cold, hard bullets. With the right aim and the right hit, the leopard would be out, permanently.

They sidled up to the house. Swept to the left. Kept cover in the overgrown grass as much as possible. Sadie had her eyes on the second window on the left side, the one crisscrossed by two boards. One yank should have those down, then they'd be inside.

"So much blood..." Sully's voice was a breath of sound behind her.

Her head moved in the slightest of nods. The coppery odor was even stronger now. The blood smelled very, very fresh. What if he had another victim in there? She could smell the traces of a human's presence. The faded wisp of perfume. A woman. *Was another victim inside*? Or was that merely the scent memory of one of those poor women he'd killed?

No time to waste.

Sadie reached the window first. But Sully's hands lifted before her. He ripped the boards away without so much as a sound.

Then it was her turn. Sadie dove through the window and landed in a crouch with her gun at the ready. Her eyes searched the darkness to find—

A large gold and black-spotted leopard. On the ground. Covered in blood. Barely moving. Gasping for breath.

Thud. Thud...

A weakening drum—his heart struggling to beat.

"Search the rest of the house!" Her order was given instantly.

Never let down your guard.

She'd learned that lesson long ago.

Sully moved like a shadow as he drifted soundlessly through the small rooms.

"Clear." His gaze swept back to the leopard. "Looks like the bastard won't be a problem much longer." He unhooked the radio on his hip and called out to Owen.

Sadie couldn't take her gaze off the leopard. Golden fur was matted red. She stepped forward. "We're with the FBI..." Why was she bothering with the whole spiel? Owen would order the beast to be killed the minute he walked into the house. Not that it looked like the leopard would live much longer anyway.

A whimper rolled from his throat. A stark cry of pain and fear.

Her nose twitched. The scent of the leopard— it wasn't *quite* right.

Not as musky as before.

But maybe the blood was just too strong.

Maybe.

"Fuck, the bastard's still alive." Owen's voice. He'd stepped into what amounted to the den of the house. Sadie turned her head and found him glaring at the trembling leopard. He'd come in alone, for the time being. Probably wanted to keep his human agents away as long as possible. Certain humans that he employed knew the supernatural score, but when it came time to battle it out against beasts, they tended to stay in the background. The better to keep living.

As she watched, Owen pushed back his jacket and reached for his gun. "This one's not going in—"

"No!" The cry burst from her lips. Some primitive instinct spurred that cry from her.

Owen's eyes widened and an *are-you-insane* look covered his face.

This scene was wrong. The leopard's scent should have been the same. But it wasn't. It had been heavier and muskier before. "Don't—don't kill him yet." Because something was *off* here.

Owen's eyebrows shot up. "Sadie, you *know* what we have to do. That piece of shit has been slicing women to bits. Rehabilitation is not going to work for him."

Yes, right, as if there were a monster rehabilitation program. No such luck. The powers that be would just rather see her kind dead.

"Why is he still in leopard form?" The fight between him and Sully had happened over fourteen hours before. The shift itself helped to speed healing for her kind. He should have transformed—

Not crawled into the house to lick his wounds and die.

"Maybe he couldn't," Owen groused. "Maybe he was hurt too badly from tangling with Sullivan."

Maybe.

But shifting after injuries like this—it was second nature. No, more than that. Survival instinct.

"Sadie..." Sully's voice was low. Worry lurked in his stare. "Don't think because he's one of yours that he can be saved."

One of yours. Her spine straightened. "He's not mine." Her kind—her family—didn't savage innocents. "Something feels *wrong.*" She shook her head. Sadie wished she could put into words why the scene made her feel so uneasy. The leopard she'd faced before had been so vicious. She'd almost smelled the evil and decay of the soul dripping from him.

This leopard was different.

Same overlying scent. Earth. Wild animal. But...not decay.

Owen aimed his gun at the leopard. Sadie put her body right in front of the gun. "Put it down."

His jaw dropped. "Sadie, you're stepping over the line—"

"Put. It. Down." He wasn't killing the leopard, not until she figured out what was happening.

Lines bracketed Owen's mouth, but he slowly lowered his weapon. "You've got two minutes, and then I'm putting a bullet in his head. No more women are dying on my watch."

Two minutes. Giving a quick nod, she spun around. She had to get closer to the shifter. The leopard's head was turned away from her. She needed to look into his eyes.

She stepped in his blood. No way to avoid it. Blood had pooled on the floor.

He wouldn't live much longer.

She kept her gun out and her body ready. If this was a ploy, he wouldn't catch her off guard.

"Stop." Sully's voice. Vibrating with barely leashed fury. "That's close enough. That shifter will *not* hurt you."

She was less than two feet away from him. Her tongue licked over desert-dry lips. "Look at me." She knew the leopard had heard every word spoken in that house. He'd heard, but hadn't reacted.

As he didn't react now.

Was he too far gone from pain?

Or part of his plan?

"If you don't look at me now," she raised her voice, injected steel, and added, "then you're going to die. Owen can fire that bullet into the back of your skull and—"

The leopard's head whipped toward her. His mouth opened in a snarl. His teeth glistened.

But his eyes were too bright. Brighter than any shifter's she'd ever seen. It almost hurt her to look into them. *Chips of emerald ice.*

"Get the hell back!" Sully roared as he reached for her.

She didn't move. Just stared into those eyes and realized that the leopard wasn't seeing her.

Eyes as blank as glass.

He wasn't seeing anything.

Blind.

She shook Sully off and dove to her knees. Her hands went to the wounds—so many wounds—and she tried to staunch the blood.

"Don't touch him!" Sully grabbed her shoulders. "Sadie, what are you—"

Her head snapped toward Sully. "Help me." She'd never asked for his help before, but she needed him now. "This isn't the same leopard."

"*What*?" Owen bellowed.

"The eyes." She swallowed. "They're green—but his are different." The leopard wasn't attacking her, damn lucky that, but his body had stiffened. *Hold on.* "His stare's too bright. Sully, he's blind." A blind shifter. He would have been born with the vision loss, because if the problem had developed later in life, the beast within would have been able to heal him. "He's *not* the one who's been killing those women." But if they couldn't help him soon, he would be the one to die that night.

Sully fell to his knees beside her. Buried his hands in the matted fur. "Fuck. What happened to him?"

She took a good look at his wounds. At the marks that could only have been made by claws. "The same thing—the same shifter—that happened to you last night."

"Christ." Owen exhaled heavily. "How many shifters are running around this city?"

Sadie didn't answer because she didn't think Owen actually wanted to hear the truth. Even though he couldn't see her, she looked back into the beast's blazing eyes. "Stay with me, okay? We're gonna help you." He had to shift to survive. "Owen, get him an ambulance. He's gonna have to be sewn up at the hospital, because when he transforms, he's not going to heal completely. One transformation won't do it. He's far too injured—"

Fur began to melt away. Muscled, golden flesh appeared as bones snapped and reshaped.

"Sonofabitch." Owen's breathless voice. Stunned. Shocked.

She guessed the guy had never seen an up-close-and-personal shift before. It was one thing to know about shifters in theory and quite another to see the bone-breaking sight for yourself.

The shifter lifted his head, no—*tried* to lift his head. Blond hair. Strong chin. High cheeks.

Sully tensed beside her. "Sadie...are you *sure?*"

She understood his doubt because the man she saw now was an exact copy of the shifter she'd seen in the bar that first night.

Same shaggy blond hair. Same strong chin. Cheeks. Nose.

An exact copy.

Except for the eyes.

If the leopard had been dead when they arrived, and those too-bright eyes had been closed, wouldn't she have thought that she'd found her killer? Yes, yes, she would have.

Sneaky bastard.

"Get the EMTs in here!" Her voice snapped like a whip. "He needs blood, stitches, and a hell of a lot of morphine!"

Owen swore and hurried outside. She heard him shouting orders.

The blond's lips trembled. Cracked, caked with blood. So many wounds still covered him. As she'd said, his injuries were far too severe to heal with one transformation. Maybe they were too severe to heal at all.

"In...no...cent..." So weak, but she heard him. Then his bright eyes closed.

"No!" Sadie screamed.

CHAPTER TWELVE

"It's the same man." Owen paced the hospital hallway. "He fits the description. He's a leopard shifter—*he's the same freaking man.*"

Sadie glanced up at him. The special agent was almost vibrating with tension.

"Lance says the smell's the same. Same scent, same man. Why the hell do we have doctors in there trying to save a sadistic killer when—"

"He's innocent." From Sully.

Sadie turned to him in surprise.

He gave her a rueful smile. "Hey, a guy doesn't forget the man who tried to kill him." He looked back at Owen. "It was a setup. We were supposed to find a dead body to satisfy us."

She nodded, not the least bit surprised that Sully had come to the same conclusion she had. They'd always been in sync on their cases. One of the reasons she'd been so drawn to him.

Their minds worked alike.

And their bodies were pure fire together.

"Should have been a perfect plan," he continued. "But the killer we're really after didn't count on that fellow—" Sully jerked his thumb toward the operating room "—fighting so hard to live."

"I figure them for twins," Sadie said. That was the only thing that made sense. A sigh escaped her as her shoulders fell.

Owen ran a shaking hand down his face. "So the killer's still out there? Hunting on Miami streets?"

Unfortunately. Yes.

"*Christ.*" He reached for his phone. Swiped his finger over the screen and blasted, "Jennings, get the men back on the streets! Now!"

Sadie watched him storm away.

"You saved his life, you know." Sully reached for her hand. "If you hadn't been there, the shifter would be dead."

Saved his life? They didn't even know if he *would* survive. "His own brother did that to him." What a nightmare. Jeez. What must life have been like for him?

But she knew. Hell. His life must have been hell.

Jacob would sooner bite off his own hand than ever hurt her.

Blind. She'd never met a leopard shifter who couldn't see. The senses were so much a part of the beast. And so necessary for hunting.

"You at least gave him a chance." Sully nodded. "Better than letting him take a bullet to the brain—which would have happened without you there. We both know Owen would have fired instantly."

Her hand turned in his grasp so that her fingers locked with his. "Thanks for backing me up."

Sully's head inclined toward her. "Don't you know yet, love, I'll always back you?"

Yes, she knew. No, she'd *thought* she knew that he'd have her back. Two years ago, she'd thought everything was perfect with him. Until he'd left her all alone in a house that smelled of him. He'd been with her so much in her home and in her bed that his scent had marked everything.

As he'd marked her.

Every day—every damn day—she'd smelled him and thought that he was lost to her. She'd grieved so much. The question she'd held back finally tore from her. "Why, Sully?"

His brows pulled low. "I don't know what makes a man cross the line and start killing—"

"No." Sadie wet her lips and rose to stand right in front of him. She had to find out the truth because she *hurt*. In her heart, the one he'd touched. Then and now. "Why did you leave me?"

Understanding flashed in his eyes even as his jaw hardened. "I didn't exactly have a choice."

She wasn't going to let him off that easily. Her shoulders stiffened. "There are always choices. You could have come to me—told me what happened—"

"And what?" His voice was harder, the Irish he could hide when he wanted rolling under the words. "Have you turn from me? Call me a monster? Have you forgotten that you tried to kill me when you realized I was a vampire?"

"If I'd wanted you dead, the stake would have been in your heart." She felt like the one who'd taken a weapon to the heart. Damaged. Broken. She'd been like that for two years. "Didn't you ever *think* about me?" Sadie couldn't believe she was even asking him the question. Where was her pride?

But she had to know. She'd thought about him—

"Every night," Sully told her flatly. "You were the last thing I thought of before sleeping and the first thing on waking."

The hole in her heart closed a bit and her breath seemed to come easier at the absolute truth she saw on his face. "But you never came back to me." Because, as he'd said before, he thought she was a human and wouldn't be able to handle him? No, it just didn't ring true, there had to be something more.

He caught her hands. Held tight to her. "Sadie, I'm not the man you remember."

No.

"After I got out of containment, I-I did things...things I never thought I'd do."

Her hands were still in his grasp, but her heart pounded too fast and she knew that with his enhanced vampire hearing, he heard the hard beats. "Tell me." The darkness was within him. She'd seen it from the beginning. Maybe, if he'd stayed just a man, the shadows in his soul would have eventually disappeared. But he wasn't just a man.

"You know the stories about the Born Masters..." No Irish lingered in his voice. Just cold, emotionless words.

And, yes, she knew about them. The vampires who'd been born, not made. The Born Masters were the ones who had the strongest psychic powers and the deadliest desires. Sadie nodded.

"Well, those tales don't even scratch the surface." An orderly walked down the hall and Sully paused, waiting until the man vanished. "The Borns can touch the minds of all they make— but it's not just through the blood link. They can *control*, sneak inside, and steal every thought you have."

Goosebumps covered her skin. She'd never encountered one of the Born Masters. Few had, and lived to spread the story.

"Ozur—"

Ozur. Oh, shit. Her claws sprang at the mention of his name. She'd heard of that ancient Viking killer. He was said to appear young, harmless. But he was really insane, bloodthirsty, and sadistic. He'd left a trail of bodies around the globe.

"He's the one who turned me that night and, later, he tried to control me."

Her heart stilled, then raced in a triple-time beat. "What did you do?" Not her Sully, he wouldn't hurt—

"I incinerated the sonofabitch."

Her breath left her in a startled rush. "What? How?" As far as she knew, only level-ten demons were strong enough to control fire to the degree needed to—

He laughed, but it was a harsh, cold rumble of sound. "I let the bastard think he had me. I drank from the prey he gave me, I hunted his enemies, and I got close. And when he rested, I fucking torched him."

Silence.

Then the intercom crackled to life as a Dr. Tom Brown was paged to ICU.

Sully dropped her hands. "Don't look at me like that."

What? She shook her head. "No, Sully, I—"

"I did what I *had* to do in order to survive. I didn't kill the prey he gave me. I let them live, Sadie, and when that prick was dead, I freed them. Yeah, I killed other vampires, I killed demons, but not innocents. *Not—*"

She rose onto her toes and kissed him. She wanted to shut off the tumble of his words and offer him the only comfort she could. *I fucking torched him.* She'd heard the agony in his voice. Knew that he'd lived through hell.

His arms swept around her and nearly crushed her with his too-strong grip. His mouth was frantic on hers. Kissing. Taking. Tongue driving between her lips.

She met him back with full passion and hunger. To know the torment he'd lived...it broke her heart.

Sully.

He ripped his mouth from hers. Breath ragged, eyes wide, he stared down at her. "You still want me?" Stunned disbelief.

What had he expected? "I'll always want you, Sully." Utter, stark truth.

His gaze, darkening, held hers. "I watched you." An admission that seemed torn from him. His fingers tightened around her as he held her in a grip that would have probably been painful for a human.

For her, it felt just right.

"October twelfth, last year, I came to you. Watched you—you were walking in the rain, just before dawn. Going to your house."

She remembered. She'd smelled him. Caught the faintest trace of his scent on the wind and ached for an hour because she'd missed him so much. She'd thought the scent was a trick of her mind.

"I'd just killed Ozur. His blood was on my hands. I wanted you so badly *but I couldn't go back to you*. I was a killer, *am* a killer, and I couldn't ask you to accept me."

Her hands pressed against his chest. Such a strong chest. Sculpted muscles. Beneath the flesh and bone, she could feel his heart pounding out a frantic rhythm that matched hers. "You don't have to ask, Sully. I want you, *all* of you."

She'd given him her blood and her body. She wasn't turning from him now.

"Sadie, I came to Miami this time because I wanted to find you. I just...I needed you. Even if you hadn't crossed my path that night—if fate hadn't sent me to you, I was coming to see you. Sometimes, I just...need to see you. Need to know that you're in the world so I can keep going."

Before she could respond, the doors of the OR flew open behind him. Sully turned at the sound, and a tall doctor in a flapping lab coat stormed toward them. His face was all angles and harsh planes. His eyes a dark silver. He pointed at them with one long finger raised. "You."

Oh, no. This couldn't be good news. Hell, if that shifter hadn't made it, then—

"Why the hell did you bring a shifter to my OR?" The doctor, whose name tag read Dr. Tidas Micco, glared at Sully.

Sadie stepped forward. After his big confession, she wanted to jump Sully and let the hot sex settle things between them, but now wasn't the time, and with the furious doc glaring at them, this was certainly not the place. "*I* brought him here." Her nostrils twitched. This doc didn't smell like a vampire or a shifter. A human? One who knew the paranormal score?

She studied him again and noticed the closely cropped black hair and high cheekbones. *Micco.* The name was vaguely familiar. Wait...Yes, yes, it clicked in her mind. She was pretty sure it was Native American. The *Other* had always heavily populated their ranks.

"You thought it was a genius plan to bring him to a human hospital?" The doctor shook his head. "What, you want him to be on the six o'clock news as a freak show?"

He was about to piss her off. A growl rumbled in her throat. His eyes widened and the doctor backed up a step. *Good move.* "We didn't have a choice," she told him, voice cool. "He was dying on us." It had been the human hospital or nothing.

"Well…" He exhaled and seemed to become a bit calmer. "You're very lucky I was on rotation tonight."

"Is he still alive?" Sully asked.

"Alive and healing at an in-freaking-credible rate." Dr. Micco rocked from one foot to the other. "You've got to get him out of here before people start asking questions."

She caught Owen's cheap-cologne scent behind her. "Will do." Her head cocked as she studied the doctor. "You know, we could use someone like you…"

Another hasty step back. "I'm not a shifter."

"No." But he knew the score, and someone like him—a man with medical training who wouldn't start screaming if he cut open a body and saw two hearts inside—he'd be a serious asset. "But you're someone who knows all about the *real* world, aren't you?"

She didn't need his grim nod for confirmation.

"I know about it, and I want to stay the hell away from it." His jaw was clenched when he gritted out, "I've seen just how much hell the *Other* can create." He jerked his thumb toward the closed doors. "He wants to see you, and I want you to get him *out* of my hospital before I have to convince any more nurses that they imagined skin sealing back up on its own."

Shifter flesh could mend itself. Not a perfect repair—the flesh would be lined with a faint red scar at the wound site, but it was still a pretty amazing trick.

A genetic trait she'd always loved.

Micco spun away from them just as Owen moved to her side. "Hey," Owen began, eyes on the doctor's retreating back, "is that the doctor who—"

"The shifter's ready to talk," Sadie cut through his words, deciding, for now, not to mention the full details of her conversation with the doctor. She knew a scared man when she saw one, and if she told Owen about the doctor right then, well, Micco's choices would be ripped away.

Like hers and Sully's had been.

Owen whistled. "That was fast. Thought for sure the cat was dead."

She was already marching toward the swinging doors with Sully at her side. "Well, you know the old saying, cats have nine lives." More than that, really.

"Yeah," Owen muttered behind her, "but I think that shifter used up about eight."

True. He'd been as close to true death as it was possible to get.

Sully's hand shoved open the green door.

They stepped inside.

And found the shifter on his feet, clothed in a loose hospital gown, with fangs bared and claws shoving from his fingertips.

Oh, hell.

No wonder the doctor was freaking out.

CHAPTER THIRTEEN

Sully's first instinct was to fight. He was about to go in punching, but Sadie stepped in front of him. Her move chilled the blood in his veins and made him realize that his lady walked on the wild side *way* too much.

"It's all right." Her voice was pitched low. "We're not here to hurt you."

The shifter's eyes—bright, glassy green—locked right on her. "I *smell* you," he spat. "I know what you are." That stare shot to Sully. "And what *you* are."

"We didn't do this to you." Sadie's voice was still low and soothing as she crept toward him. They were lucky because all of the nurses and doctors had cleared out, probably courtesy of Dr. Micco. "*We* didn't hurt you," she added carefully.

"I know who the hell did this to me!" Fury. Pain. "The same bastard who has spent thirty years trying to kill me. Thirty damn years." His blond head shook. "He didn't succeed before, and he *won't*."

Sully kept his attention fully locked on the shifter. Sadie might feel pity for the man, but Sully knew a wounded beast was one seriously *dangerous* beast. One most likely to bite off the hand that wanted to help him.

Sully didn't intend to let anyone else bite Sadie. If he had to throw the shifter across the room to protect her, he was more than ready for the job.

She still wants me. She'd looked at him with honest desire in her eyes. She knew the truth about him, and she still wanted him. Hell, no, Sully wasn't about to let anyone hurt so much as a single hair on her gorgeous head.

"Ease up, shifter," he ordered, aware of Owen stumbling to a stop behind him. "We pulled your body out of that house and saved your hide."

"Hell. I knew we should have killed him when we had the chance." Owen's quiet mutter.

The shifter's head snapped up. "What?" His nostrils flared. "*You.* You're the trigger-happy moron."

Uh-oh. Looked like the fellow hadn't been quite as out of it as they'd thought.

Silence followed his charge. The uncomfortable kind.

Then Owen brushed past Sully. Sully lifted his brows but made no move to stop the man. If Owen wanted a beating, fine by him.

"I'm Special Agent Owen Miller, cat. And, yes, I'm the one who almost put a bullet in your head." His right hand brushed back his jacket to reveal his weapon. As if the gun would help him.

Didn't Owen understand that if the shifter decided to attack, he'd never have time to so much as draw his weapon?

Apparently not because Owen continued, "When I've got dead women in the city, *butchered* women, I don't play nicely. The last vic is alive, thank Christ, but—"

The shifter was on him in an instant. "Su is alive?" Hope had his face lighting up like some kind of freaking Christmas tree as he clung tightly to Owen.

Ah. Sadie glanced back and met Sully's gaze. One of her eyebrows crooked up.

He gave a slight nod. They both realized the shifter was *way* into this Su.

"Sully saved her," Sadie said as she focused back on the shifter. "She's in this hospital, recovering and—"

"What the hell?" Owen shook off the shifter's hold and glowered at Sadie. "Why are you telling him this stuff?"

"Because now that I've shared with him, he's going to tell us some information." She crossed her arms over her chest. "Aren't you, shifter? Tit for tat. If you wanna know about the vic, you tell us about the beast who tried to slice you open."

Tried? The guy *had been* sliced open.

The shifter's shoulders fell. He turned around, paced a few steps away, and gave Sully an unfortunate view of his arse, courtesy of the gaping gown.

Sully glanced over and found Sadie getting the same view. He snarled. She didn't need to be eyeing another man's—

The shifter spun back around. "He—he's my brother. Corey Blaine." He gestured to his face.

"Twin brother, but I guess you already knew that, huh?"

Sully stared into the face that was the perfect reflection of a killer's. "He set you up—*you* know that, right? He wanted us to find your body and think that you were the killer."

A nod.

"Where is he?" Sadie demanded.

"I don't know, I—"

"He has to have a safe house around here. Friends. Hunting grounds," she pushed relentlessly. "Tell us. We can't let another woman die!"

"Dammit, I know that!" His hands shot into the air. "Don't you think I fucking hate him? He took Su!"

"Just who is this Su to you?" Owen probed. "A lover?"

"She could have been." His shoulders fell. "She could have been...everything."

Almost helplessly, Sully's gaze drifted to Sadie.

Everything. Aye, he knew what that was like. He could sure as hell relate. Sully's gaze returned to the shifter.

"Now, she'll never be mine." Desolation washed across his face. "Because of my own brother!"

"Where is he?" Sadie asked her question again.

"I don't know." His lips pressed together for a moment, then he rasped, "Hiding. Waiting. Getting ready to watch the news and see the story about the dead body that was found—*my* body."

A story he wouldn't see, and when it didn't air, he'd become enraged.

"You're coming with us," Owen announced as he squared his shoulders. "Until this perp is out of commission and I know for absolute certain that you weren't involved."

"Involved? I'm not a killer!"

"Sure you are." Owen glanced from his face to the claws that were still out. "Everyone is, human and *Other,* deep inside. All that matters is how much of a push it takes to get the killer to come out."

Sully knew that, for once, Owen spoke the truth.

"You'll stay under guard," Owen continued curtly. "Until your brother's body is at my feet."

***

They took the shifter to a safe house, one surrounded by guards who were *Other.*

"You should have everything you need." Sadie tossed a suitcase onto the floor near their new charge—his name was Kyle. Kyle Blaine. Owen had sent an agent out to get clothes for him so the guy should now be well supplied.

Sully waited for her just outside the room. She hesitated. She knew she should go but—

"You don't have to pity me." Kyle's shoulders were stiff as he stood with his back to her. He wore green scrubs that Dr. Micco had provided before they left the hospital.

At his low words, her eyebrows shot up. "I don't pity you." Wait, that wasn't entirely true.

Kyle's brother was a sadistic killer who'd tried to kill him. He'd gotten screwed on the family end. *He got a killer, while I got a brother who faced off with a devil to protect me.*

"I might not be able to see, but it doesn't mean I'm weak." Harsh, rumbling words.

Her lips parted in surprise as she understood what he was saying. "Hold on. You need to back up a bit. No, it's not because of—"

He whirled toward her and his eyes zeroed instantly on to her face. "You're five-foot-two, one hundred fifteen pounds. You've got blond hair, you use rose-scented shampoo, and you've been fucking the vampire who is pacing outside the door."

She blinked. Well, someone was certainly dead on target.

"I can't see, but I can hear, smell, taste, and feel everything just fine."

Yes, shifters had incredible senses. She certainly understood that. Hers were far, far superior to any human's.

"My remaining senses are stronger than other shifters'." Said simply. "It's like they kicked into high gear to make up for my eyes."

She'd heard about something like that happening with humans.

"I don't need sight—no, forget that." He drew in a deep breath and stalked forward and only stopped when he was inches away from her. "I was lying earlier, I *can* see, I just don't use my broken eyes to do it."

"*Sadie*." Sully's voice.

Her head whipped toward him. He stood in the doorway. His face was locked into tense lines and his black eyes were on Kyle.

She held up her hand. "It's okay, Sully." Time for truth. Her head turned back toward the shifter. "And I was lying, too, Kyle."

His lips parted. "I *knew*—"

"I pity you because you had the shit-screwed luck to be born with that jerk as your brother. That really sucks, and I'm sorry that he hurt you." Kyle had probably been hurt more than he would ever reveal. "But I don't pity you for any other reason." She'd be a fool if she did. She could *feel* the shifter's power. "Got it?"

Maybe someone else would think that a shifter without vision was weak, but she knew her kind too well. No shifter was weak. Ever. They were the most dangerous hunters in the world.

And she pitied anyone who thought otherwise.

He exhaled and some of the tension seemed to drain from his shoulders. "Got it."

"Good." She stepped to the side. "If you think of anything else to tell us, Agent Moody's outside." The giant demon with the flame tattoos was a very fine guard. "Let him know and he'll get word to Sully or me."

Sully wasn't looking particularly happy right then. He stood in the doorway, filling the space, and his burning glare stayed focused on Kyle.

Sadie headed for her vamp.

"Do you...know how she is?" It sounded like the words had been ripped from Kyle.

Sadie didn't have to ask who "she" was. "Su hasn't woken up yet." Su Kent, the victim Sully had managed to rescue.

Su Kent, age thirty-two. Art director at the Miami Museum. Her mother had immigrated from Thailand and married Jonathan Kent, an ex-Marine.

"Is she going to make it?" he asked gruffly

"I think so." She hoped so. Owen had checked the vic out thoroughly. From all accounts, Su was a genuinely good person, a pretty rare thing. She donated food to the needy and taught an after-school art program for disadvantaged kids. The woman had never even gotten so much as a parking ticket.

A nice lady. One who sure hadn't deserved the horror she'd suffered.

Sadie walked toward Sully. No, Su hadn't deserved her fate. Just like Sully hadn't deserved the horror that had happened to him and his team.

Sometimes, life truly sucked.

"I'll help you." Kyle's rushed words had her glancing back at him. "I want Corey stopped. My whole life, my parents hated me because of the way I was. They said I was weak."

The pain on his face was gut-wrenching.

"Corey made my life *hell*. You don't know what he did all those years—" Kyle broke off with a shake of his head. "Doesn't matter."

But she thought it did.

"*I* survived," he said grimly. "But he's not going to. Not this time."

"We'll stop him," Sadie promised, and she absolutely meant those words. "He's not going to hurt anyone else."

Yes, they would stop the leopard—once they *found* him.

***

The shifter whore was with the vampire again. Walking with him, letting him wrap his arm around her shoulders, body pressed to body.

She was with the parasite, all but purring up at him.

She knew better.

He snarled and lowered his binoculars.

Binoculars—a human invention, one that was coming in handy. He couldn't risk getting close enough for the female shifter to smell him or close enough for his freak of a brother to catch his scent with that hyped-up nose of his.

Should have cut off Kyle's nose years ago. Should have killed him years ago.

Of course, he'd tried, and nearly succeeded more times than he could count. But Kyle had always managed to survive. Somehow. Lucky bastard. That luck wouldn't last forever. Corey would make sure of it.

This last time, *she'd* been the one to save his brother. Sadie Townsend. Tough agent. Sexy bitch.

Soon-to-be dead woman.

The vampire bent and pressed a kiss to her temple.

The binoculars seemed to explode in his hand. Glass, metal, and blood fell from his fingers. *Blood.*

Sadie had given her blood to the vampire. Freely given blood and body. She wasn't a worthy adversary like he'd originally thought. She wasn't a shifter of skill to fight and challenge.

She was garbage. A whore who'd spread her legs too quickly for the undead.

She'd pay for that. Pay for desecrating their kind. It was time for the hunt to come to an end.

Time for Sadie Townsend to die.

***

He wouldn't lose her.

Sully held Sadie close. His arm was curled tightly around her shoulders as they hurried up the steps to her house.

The desolation on Kyle's face when he'd asked about his Su—

No, that *wasn't* the end Sully would have with Sadie. He wasn't giving her up. Wasn't going to live his life—such as it was—without her.

The instant the door shut behind them, his mouth was on hers. The need and the consuming lust had his body shaking. His cock was rock hard, fully erect, and ready to thrust into her tight sex.

Her lips and tongue met his with the same feverish intensity. He could taste the hunger in her kiss. They both felt the same frantic fever of desire.

Fuck, yes.

She clawed at his shirt and shredded the material so that her hands could get to his skin. Her fingers curled over his muscles, and her hot hands that sent sparks dancing over his body.

A purr rumbled in her throat, and his cock jerked in hungry anticipation.

Her fingers darted down to the buckle of his belt.

Sully ripped his mouth from hers. "No!"

Her eyes widened. So gold. And her lips were so red and wet and—

He picked her up, took five steps into the dining room, and spread her out on the table. *Fucking beautiful.* He'd wanted to make a meal of her all night.

Her lips curved in a slow smile as she kicked off her shoes.

I'd die for her. The realization hit him as he watched her gorgeous smile. Lie. Kill. Die. Anything she wanted. He was lost. And so desperate for her. He'd always be desperate.

He caught the waist of her pants. Jerked the soft cotton down, and, at the same time, he snagged the scrap of lace that shielded her sex.

Sadie tossed her shirt away and unhooked her bra, revealing those perfect lick-me breasts.

He caught her nipple with his mouth. Sucked and licked and tasted the sweetness that was his Sadie. The scent of her arousal filled the air around him. Rich. Tempting.

Her hands were on his back. Stroking and pulling him closer.

Sully freed her breast, only to immediately turn his attention to the other pink nipple. She tasted so *good*.

And he was going to taste more. So much more.

He licked his lips when he rose. "Spread your legs."

The table was a dark cherry beneath her, making her skin seem to shine in stark contrast.

Her legs parted, revealing the plump, pink folds of her aroused flesh. Pink and wet and perfect.

Sully's mouth captured her. Pressed tight to that sweet center and *took*. His tongue and lips teased her. Pushed against the button of her desire. Tasted the silky heaven open to him.

Sully took from her like a man starving because he was. The more he tasted, the more he hungered. His tongue drove into her body. The need for her essence burned to his very soul.

He heard her shout of release. Felt the ripples of her climax.

Still he took. His Sadie. His. Forever.

"Sully!" Sadie called out his name even as she tugged at his hair. "Th-this time...you...inside."

His cock was about to explode so that sounded like a damn brilliant idea to him. One final swipe of his tongue, then—

He shoved his jeans down. Caught his cock in one hand and pushed the broad head between her thighs.

Sully sank into her. Their eyes met. He withdrew. Thrust deep.

Her breath choked out. He could see the edge of her teeth.

Her muscles clamped around him.

So. Damn. Tight.

They climaxed together. The release slammed through them. Sully held her tight, drinking the cries from her lips and knowing that he'd found—

Everything.

All he'd ever wanted—all he could ever want—he'd found it all with his Sadie. He held her tight. Cradled her. Treasured her. And wondered...

Dammit...why, *why* couldn't a monster have a chance at love?

***

Someone was pounding at the door. Sadie blinked awake. She forced the sleep from her eyes so that she could glare at the bedside clock. Ten fifteen.

Not exactly the crack of dawn, but then, she hadn't gotten to sleep until after six that morning.

An arm rested over her stomach. A strong thigh caged her legs.

She smiled when she caught sight of Sully's tousled hair. He liked to hold her when he slept. She rather enjoyed that. Made her feel...wanted. Ah, that was—

"Agent Townsend! Dammit, Sadie, I know you hear me! Freaking cat ears—you probably heard me drive up!" The pounding of a fist rattled her door, then Owen shouted, "Get your clothes on and open this door! We've got a situation—"

"That man needs an ass kicking," she muttered.

"Yeah, he does," Sully growled.

Sadie smiled and kissed his bare shoulder before she managed to slide free of his grasp. She grabbed her robe and belted it quickly. "Remind me to give him one."

Sully didn't get out of the bed. Not that she blamed him. Daylight and vampires really didn't mix well. His kind were weaker when the sun rose, often suffering headaches and nausea—no wonder they preferred the nightlife.

She hurried across the room and took the stairs three at a time. Adrenaline already kicked through her blood. When Sadie jerked open her front door, Owen was still shouting.

His eyes widened when he saw her. His stare swept from her hair—and, oh, yeah, she knew it had to look wild, courtesy of Sully's fingers—to her bare thighs. Her silky black robe was short because she hated having her legs trapped by too much fabric. Leopards sometimes had confinement issues.

But she didn't mind it when Sully held her tight in bed. No, she didn't mind that confinement at all.

Owen drew in a hard breath. "What? Do you spend all your free time screwing vampires?"

Ass kicking. Her hands dropped to her sides. One more minute, and she'd let her claws out. She hadn't gotten enough sleep for this crap. "Do you spend all your time being a prick?"

Owen blinked. Then scraped a hand over his face. "Yeah, unfortunately, I pretty much do."

What?

His gaze drifted over her shoulder as he frowned. "Tell Sleeping Beauty to wake his butt up, I need him."

"Daytime's not exactly his peak performance time." *A fact Owen knew.*

"I don't need his strength." Owen looked back at her. "I need his contacts."

Her brow furrowed. Behind her, she heard the creak of the stairs. Sounded like Sully was coming to join their little party. "What's happening?" Sadie asked. She stepped back because she knew she had to let Owen inside.

The door closed behind him with a soft click. "Su Kent's awake and, unfortunately, her memory of the attack is crystal clear."

Sadie winced. Uh-oh. "Has she...started telling the hospital staff about what happened?" If she had, Su would either be headlining the news soon or she'd find herself shipped off to the psych ward for the foreseeable future.

"She told Dr. Micco. He was in the room when she opened her eyes and started screaming about men with claws and fangs."

A soft footfall whispered behind her. A moment later, Sully's hand pressed against her back. "What do you want me to do? I can't make her forget. You know I can't work Thrall yet."

Thrall. The old vamp term for the ability to control a victim's mind. To get the unwilling to surrender, to bare a throat and beg to be Taken.

Born Masters had the ability with their first kill. For others, age brought the power, and, in terms of a vamp's age, Sully was still a newborn.

Though not quite as defenseless.

"We need help from a demon. Moody has some contacts, but they aren't exactly being helpful."

Yes, well, Sadie knew Moody wasn't overly popular among his kind. Demons didn't tend to think too highly of anybody who looked or acted like a cop. And Moody had been a cop for ten years before joining the Bureau.

"Do you know any demons who owe you a favor?" Owen pushed.

Sadie glanced back at Sully. Dealing in favors—the way of the human world and the *Other*.

Sully nodded. "A few."

"Good, because you're gonna have to call in those debts today."

Sully lifted his hand and pressed his fingers against his forehead. "What do you need?" What, not who. He knew the game.

Owen flashed his shark's smile. "A level-eight or nine demon. The stronger, the better."

Level-eight or nine. Sadie exhaled slowly. Demon power was on a scale from one to ten. The low-level demons—the ones to threes—were barely any threat to the human population. It was the high-level demons that everyone feared. Those above a level seven distinction, or L7, were trouble.

Powerful. Deadly.

Level tens—they were the hell-on-earth guys with their supernatural powers. But a level nine—well, he or she sure wouldn't be someone to take lightly. Especially considering that a demon with that much power might be able to rip away the mind of a human.

"You sure about this?" she asked Owen.

"There's no choice. We need help. Someone has to make Ms. Kent forget all about her trip to hell."

A perfect job for a demon.

CHAPTER FOURTEEN

The woman on the bed was covered in stark white bandages. Her straight black hair fell around her face, and her dark eyes blazed with fear.

"I know you." Her voice was a broken rasp.

Sully hesitated just inside the doorway. "Do you now?" Aye, that was part of the problem.

A tear leaked from her left eye and she began to shake, then to scream, with a voice long gone hoarse. Horrible, gasping gurgles sprang from her throat.

"The bastard tortured her for hours," Owen revealed, shaking his head. He stood at the foot of Su Kent's bed with his hands clenched behind his back. "Micco wants to send her to a psych ward—"

Where Sully knew she'd probably stay for a long, long time. Especially if she started talking about men who could become real monsters.

Su stopped screaming and fell back against the mattress. Sully noticed the straps that were tied to her wrists, anchoring her to the bed. He took a cautious step forward.

She flinched and turned her head away. "S-stop...M-make it all...st-stop..." Her pain and fear filled the room.

I'll find the leopard. And I'll stop him from hurting anyone else ever again.

"Su," Sully said her name quietly.

Another man stepped into the room behind him and the door closed almost soundlessly.

The woman on the bed didn't move.

"*Su.*" Sully walked around the bed. Stopped beside her and saw that her dark eyes were open, but staring at nothing. No, staring at a nightmare only *she* could see.

He reached for her hand. Damn. She was cold.

Her lips parted and Sully was afraid the woman was about to start screaming again.

"I never hurt you." He spoke to her as another tear rolled down her cheek. She stared right through him. "I hurt *him*. I stopped *him* before he could do anything else to you."

"Cl-claws...and t-teeth..." Dry heaves shook her chest.

Sully swallowed and wondered if she was talking about the shifter or him.

"I didn't hurt you," he repeated, trying to reach her. He wished that Sadie was there. She always had a much softer touch than he did. But Owen had sent her back out to that damn bloody building downtown. He'd wanted Sadie and her team to canvas the area to see if anyone knew anything about Corey Blaine—and to make certain the killer hadn't left any telling tracks that would help them nail him.

Sadie was the best hunter they had. She hadn't been with the unit that swept the building the night before, and Owen was worried as hell they'd missed something without her.

But I sure could have used her help here. With her soothing voice and understanding eyes, she would have been able to reach the shattered Su.

"Hurt...I-I hurt...s-so much. C-can't forget..."

"Do you want to?" He knew Owen's attention was locked on them. Her response was very, very important.

Her head moved in the briefest of nods.

Not good enough. Owen wanted him to help wipe out Su's memories. Before he gave the demon standing so still next to the door the all clear, Sully wanted to make absolutely certain Su understood what was happening.

She'd have a choice in this, no matter what Owen wanted.

"Tell me, Su. Tell me what you want."

"T-to for...get..." Her swollen lips trembled. "Go back...like before."

It wouldn't be exactly like before.

But it wouldn't be like surviving hell, either.

"I can do that. I can take all the bad memories away."

Her hand twisted and grabbed his with desperate strength. Her eyes finally locked on his. No, finally *saw* him. "Do it." The clearest thing she'd said.

The choice was made.

The demon stepped forward.

***

The building reeked of the leopard. Sadie stood outside the old building on Burns and Montay, her nose wrinkling. That jerk had left his scent *everywhere.*

"Probably living here," she said to the two men at her back. Humans, but men she trusted. Men she'd worked with before. "His stench is too strong."

"Crime scene guys found traces of blood in two other rooms on the second floor." This came from Derek Martin, the blond agent who liked to keep one hand close to his gun at all times. Smart fellow. "Matched it to Donna Summers and Theresa Kite."

The first two victims. No, the two victims they *knew* about. Sadie was sure there'd been more. Corey Blaine hadn't been a good little choirboy his whole life. There'd been other kills, those he'd kept secret, but in Miami, he'd stopped hiding the bodies.

Cocky asshole. Taunting the cops and scaring the humans.

"So this is where he brought his prey." The sun was starting to set, and the red glow fell over the building like a shadow made of blood.

She'd already walked the streets for most of the day. Talked to every person she could find in the area, but no one remembered Corey Blaine. Odd. It wasn't like the fellow was easy to forget.

"We're going over this building," she announced. "Every single room." *Every single inch.* Six stories, twelve rooms per floor. Sure, the building had been searched three times already—

But not by her.

Her nostrils flared. That scent was driving her crazy. The leopard sure had marked his turf. "Let's get this done." Her stomach was in knots. "I want to find this perp." She had to find him and stop him before he tortured and killed another woman.

***

The straps were gone from Su's wrists. She lay against the mattress, seemingly calm. The tears on her cheeks were drying.

"That it?" Owen asked, frowning at the demon.

Charles Lamoyne gave a nod, then glanced at Sully. "You're in *my* debt now, Sullivan."

Fabulous. Just where he wanted to be, owing a demon. Sully inclined his head.

"I'll collect payment one of these days." A smile from Charles. Not the friendly kind. "Count on it."

He would.

Charles turned away and headed for the door.

It had taken a big chunk of the day to find the demon. He wasn't one to advertise his presence in the city. Most of the strongest *Other* liked to keep to the shadows. The better to watch the game mortals played.

Lamoyne hadn't helped the human out of the goodness of his heart. As far as Sully knew, there wasn't much goodness in there. But Sully had saved Lamoyne's hide a year ago, when he'd stopped a human under Thrall from taking the demon's head.

He'd hoped for an even debt exchange.

Sully should have known he'd have to pay a bit more for the help. Most demons didn't do favors for humans. Lamoyne had made a big exception by helping Su.

Sully glanced back at the woman. Her eyes were closing, and she looked almost...peaceful.

Maybe she'd stay that way.

Lamoyne's psychic talent was shading memories and twisting truth. When Su woke up again, she'd have images from a car wreck in her mind. Perfect memories to match her injuries.

She'd remember the squeal of tires and the crunch of metal—

But not the claws of monsters.

Sully turned away from her. He was bone tired, but, luckily, the sun would be down soon.

Maybe the headache pounding at the front of his skull would end when the night came.

Hmmm...or maybe, while he was in the hospital, he should take a quick swing by the nearest blood bank for a little pick-me-up. He was sure there was a nice, refrigerated supply of his favorite liquid close by.

***

When Sadie stepped onto the second floor, every muscle in her body tightened.

Blood and death were in the air. So thick she nearly choked.

Sully had fought here. Women had died. And that sick freak had played.

His stench was so much stronger here. Her eyes narrowed. Stronger...and fresher.

Her claws burst from her fingertips.

***

Sully froze just outside of the elevator bank at Hudson Hospital.

For an instant, he could have sworn that he'd caught a whiff of Sadie's scent.

But, no, that was crazy. She wasn't even close by. She was on the other side of town, searching that old building.

A whisper of fear seemed to brush over his body. A spike of anger surged in his blood. And he knew—

Blood link.

Hell.

The fear and anger were Sadie's.

Something is wrong. Sadie needs me!

***

He attacked her first. The fully shifted leopard sprang from the room on the left and swiped his claws across her stomach. Sadie fell onto the floor, hard, and heard gunshots blast around her as the two agents fired. Her skin burned, blood soaked her shirt, and she knew that she was in serious trouble.

Lying in wait.

Leopards were patient hunters. Corey Blaine had known she'd come to find him.

A man's scream erupted from close by.

Gritting her teeth, she tried to rise. She managed to get to her knees, and she pulled out her gun. She'd save the claws and teeth this time. A bullet would work great.

The leopard was crouched over Derek, with *his* claws less than an inch away from the man's throat.

The second agent, Collier Duwane, sprawled on the floor. His eyes were closed.

The leopard's ears twitched. His claws moved in for the kill.

"No!" Her yell was guttural. She could take the shot, but Derek might still die. Those claws were too close to him.

Shit.

The leopard snarled at her.

Her fingers tightened around the gun. Without the weapon, *she* was a dead woman. There wouldn't be enough time to shift before he attacked.

Sully. She needed him.

Her gaze dropped to Derek. His neck was twisted to the side, and he stared at her. Horrified realization filled his eyes.

Do it. He mouthed the words.

But she didn't pull the trigger. If she pulled it, the leopard's claws would still rip into Derek. He'd die. And if she dropped her weapon, the leopard would attack her. *After* he slashed Derek from ear to ear.

He's going to kill Derek no matter what.

No. No, Derek was on her team. She wasn't going to let him die. She couldn't let him—

The leopard roared.

So did Sadie.

Then she fired.

The bullet hit the leopard dead center in his outstretched paw, exploding through muscle and bone, then slamming into the wall just beyond the beast. Derek managed to roll to the side, and he pushed to his feet. Yet just as Derek staggered upright, the leopard rammed into him. The agent's head hit the wall. Down he went.

Sadie fired again. She hadn't been able to aim for the leopard's head or heart with the first bullet, and he was moving too fast now to get a clear shot. *Dammit.* Only a shot in the head or heart would stop him. So she fired—again and again.

The leopard sprang at her, and the beast within Sadie clawed for her freedom.

***

Sadie.

For a moment, her image swam before Sully. A white-hot lance of pain exploded across his chest. Sully swore he could feel the cold splash of blood.

Then—nothing.

Terror had his heart nearly stopping. The blood link between them had grown so strong that he knew what was happening to her. He was losing Sadie.

Hell, no.

Sully forgot about the elevator and ran for the stairs. Screw the sunlight that was still fighting the night. Sadie needed him.

A ghrá, hold on. Please, hold on. He had to get to Sadie. Had to help her. She was the only thing of value in his world. The only person who mattered.

The only woman he'd ever loved.

Hold on.

***

A red haze filled her vision. Blood. Hers. His. Her leopard was in control of Sadie now, and she was fighting for her life—

And the lives of her two agents.

Pain was constant. The attack from Corey Blaine had been vicious. The prick outweighed her by a good forty pounds in animal form, and he had insanity on his side, always an advantage for a killer.

But she wasn't powerless. Sadie had her rage and her desperate desire to stay alive fueling her. So she fought him. Every slash of his claws led to an assault from hers. She wasn't letting him leave this room. He *wouldn't* kill again.

His teeth clamped on to her shoulder.

And another growl rumbled from the doorway.

Through the fury, she saw him, coming like an avenging angel—no, more like a pissed-off devil.

Another leopard. Golden fur lined with the dark rosettes of her kind. His mouth opened in a snarl. His teeth glistened with saliva. She recognized his scent immediately, even before she saw his glassy stare.

Kyle.

He launched across the room. His hind legs kicked back to send him soaring. His teeth locked on to Corey, ripped and tore, and the coppery scent of blood deepened.

Sadie took a moment, panting and gathering her strength. This was it. She could feel the approaching kill in the air. No escape. Corey Blaine was about to answer for his crimes.

And when he arrived in hell, she didn't think the devil was gonna cut him any slack.

Her whiskers quivered as she leaned down in a crouch. She waited for the perfect moment to join the growling, biting blur that was the other two leopards.

Now. She shot forward, teeth and claws ready.

Together, she and Kyle took the killer down, and his furious cries echoed around them until—

Silence.

Then the snap of bones.

Sadie and Kyle slowly eased back. The battle was over. The beaten leopard had shifted. An automatic survival instinct. Corey's wounds were deep. His choice was either shift or die.

When the transformation was over, Corey flopped naked on the floor. His breath choked out in labored heaves.

Sadie let the white-hot fire of the change sweep over her. Corey wasn't in any shape to attack now. She had to check on her men and get them an ambulance ASAP. She didn't care about her nudity. Her clothes had shredded when she'd shifted into the cat. She'd been badly wounded, was still hurt—the shift had far from healed her completely—but thanks to her rush of adrenaline, the injuries barely slowed her down. Kyle was snarling over his brother, so that situation seemed under control. Now her priority was her men. Men who looked like they were stepping too close to the cold door of death.

Derek groaned. He tried to raise his arm, but his hand dropped back to the floor. Sadie scrambled around him. She searched desperately to find the phone she'd lost when she'd shifted. *Ambulance.* Humans couldn't survive this kind of assault without help. She had to get an ambulance—

The quiet *snick* of a gun's safety release whispered in her ears. She turned, too slowly, and saw that Corey had somehow managed to get a gun. In a split second, she recognized it as Derek's weapon. She'd seen it fly across the room earlier, then forgotten about it in the snap of teeth and the swipe of claws.

Still in leopard form, Kyle roared and swiped with his claws just as Corey fired at him.

The bullet thudded into Kyle's body. The leopard fell.

Then, smiling, bleeding, Corey turned the gun on her—

And he fired again.

***

Sully froze just outside the building on Montay. All of the breath left his lungs in a rush, and fire exploded in the middle of his chest. The pain drove him to his knees.

A pain that wasn't his.

No.

He tried to rise, but fell onto the cement. "*Sadie.*" She was slipping away from him. He knew it, and the pain seemed to rip his heart apart.

He'd reached her too late.

Tires squealed behind him. Doors slammed.

"Sullivan? *Sullivan!*" Owen grabbed Sully and jerked him to his feet.

The pain began to fade and an icy numbness took its place. He stared up at the building. It was now covered by the darkness of night.

"Is Sadie here?" Owen demanded. "We can't get her team to answer us, there's no contact—"

Owen's voice was buzzing in his ear.

She was there. He could feel her. But for how long? She was hurt, badly hurt, and he knew the cruel bitch that was fate was trying to steal his Sadie away.

Not going to fucking happen.

CHAPTER FIFTEEN

He'd never forget his first sight of that room. The blood. The bodies.

Sadie positioned on the floor like a broken doll. Her lashes still against her too-white cheeks.

He fell to his knees beside her. Touched her face. Slowly, so slowly, her lashes lifted. Her golden eyes were full of so much pain.

"Sh-shot her..."

His head whipped up at the hoarse whisper. Kyle Blaine was pushing himself off the floor. "M-missed my h-heart..." Sully saw the hole in his chest. Damn, weren't shifters supposed to heal from—

"B-but he got h-hers..."

The room spun. No, no that wasn't possible. Sadie hadn't been shot in the heart. He'd know, he'd—

Hear the rush of her blood spilling out. The broken beat as her heart struggled. The bullet had clipped the side of her heart. Too damaged. It couldn't work. Weakening.

"B-bastard's d-dead now...."

Sully didn't even glance toward the body. He could smell the stench of death.

"B-but he-he got h-her," Kyle rasped. "S-sorry—"

"The hell he did!" Sully's arms were tight around her. He wouldn't look at her chest. No, he didn't want to see the wound, but he could *feel* it, as if his own chest had been ripped open. "You're not goin' anywhere, Sadie, you hear me?" He was rocking her, back and forth, faster and faster.

Her eyes were open, but she didn't seem to see him. Her gaze was frozen. Her breath barely seemed to whisper past her pale lips.

How the hell is she even still alive? The question blasted through his mind. Terrified him.

But he knew the answer. His Sadie lived because she had a shifter's strength. Right then, he thanked the God he'd forgotten two years ago, then Sully whispered a prayer for his forgiveness.

Because he knew what he was going to do.

"*A ghrá,* stay with me." His fingers brushed over her neck. His head lowered and his mouth hovered over her throat.

Would she want this life?

An insidious whisper. One that came from deep within. One that he ignored.

His teeth pressed against her skin. The blood flowed faster from her wounds now, but the scent didn't tempt him.

It scared the hell out of him.

"Sadie..." No more time to waste. Soon, she wouldn't have any blood left to take.

His teeth pierced her neck. Blood trickled onto his tongue.

Sadie. Please don't leave me.

"What the hell are you doing, Sullivan?" Owen grabbed him and tried to force Sully to release his hold on Sadie. "That's not what she wants—"

Sully raised his head. A rumble rolled in his throat. He wasn't about to let her go. "Fuck off!" His cry erupted as a scream of fury that shook the room. "She's not dying. She's too strong. She's—"

Needed too much. Sadie was needed too much. Loved too much.

He'd just found her again. How was he supposed to live for centuries without her?

No. No, he couldn't. He was a selfish bastard, and he wanted his Sadie. He wanted her with him. Wanted her smiles and her laughter and—

"She doesn't *want* this." Absolute certainty from Owen. "We can get her to a hospital. They can stitch her up. Fix her until she's strong enough to heal—"

"She's got less than a minute left." Sully's voice broke. He lifted her. Cradled her as gently as he could. With shaking fingers, Sully pushed her head toward his throat. Her cool lips skimmed over his skin. "I *feel* her leaving. If she were human, she'd have died when the bullet drove into her."

He knew Sadie. Pure shifter will had kept her alive. The beast inside fighting a battle to heal. A battle that couldn't be won.

Too much blood loss.

"You can't do this!" Owen raged.

Why was Owen getting a conscience?

"Dammit, Sullivan, she doesn't want—"

"I know what she fuckin' wants!" He knew...and what he knew tore his guts apart.

Sadie wanted her beast. The leopard within that had been a part of her since birth. The leopard that would die if he turned her. He knew the stories. He'd heard all the legends. A shifter lost the power to transform when she was reborn as a vampire.

That life ended, and a new one began.

"Sadie..." Sully breathed her name as pain gutted him.

Choices.

Piss. This damn life—always about choices.

He wouldn't take her choice away. His had been taken away. He wouldn't do the same thing to Sadie. Not his Sadie. Because, yes, he was a selfish bastard...except...when it came down to the very end. With her.

With Sadie...*she* had to always come first.

But he couldn't just sit there and let her die.

Fucking hell—don't leave me! A cry that shook his soul.

"L-live..." Gasped out. Weak.

His eyes widened. He tilted Sadie's chin back. He stared into the golden eyes that *saw* him and held agony. "Sadie?"

"L-live..." Sadie managed once again. Her voice little more than a breath.

Sadie Townsend was the strongest woman he'd ever met—and she was a fighter, until death and beyond. She was choosing—him and life, with seconds to spare.

He offered his throat to her, guided her head because she was too weak, and a moment later, Sully felt the sharp sting of her teeth.

Live.

Sadie took his blood...and died.

CHAPTER SIXTEEN

Very, very slowly, Sadie opened her eyes. She found herself lying on a soft bed—her bed. The lights were off and darkness cloaked the room. But she could see perfectly.

Her nostrils flared. She caught the scent of flowers. The fabric softener she used on her sheets. The vanilla-scented candle she kept in the living room.

She raised her hand to her chest and found the skin healed.

She'd survived. Part of her had, anyway.

Her fangs were out and the hunger, a great, gnawing hunger for food—no, *blood*—had her belly clenching.

The bedroom door squeaked open, and her gaze flew across the room to zero in on Sully.

He stared at her, not speaking, and she could see the worry on his face.

Her hands clenched around the sheets.

"Sadie…" He shook his head. "Do you know what happened? Do you know—"

"That I'm a vampire?" Yes, she knew. She remembered everything. Every horrifying moment. She could still feel the twisted thud of her heart. *Broken.* She'd known death was coming for her, and while she didn't fear the other side or what waited, she hadn't wanted to leave.

It had been too soon.

In that moment, when the fog had cleared from her eyes and she'd seen Sully gazing down at her with such fear on his face, she'd known she would have traded anything, *everything,* she had to stay with him.

Even her beast.

And she had.

"It's not as bad as you think. You don't have to kill to live. You can get blood from a hospital." He swallowed, then added, "You're not linked to any other vampires, just me. You have no Born Master who can control you. You'll be as strong as before—you just...have to take it easier during the daytime." He crossed to her side as the words poured out of him. "You're still the same, Sadie, you're—"

"I can't shift." Spoken quietly.

His jaw clenched. "No, no, you can't."

"But I'm alive." Some might disagree with that. Screw them. Sadie forced her fingers to ease their death grip, and she reached for him. "I'm alive, and I'm with you." She'd made her choice.

She'd made it before Corey Blaine had taken aim on her in that room.

She'd decided last night when she'd spooned in bed with Sully, his arms around her. She'd known that she never wanted to leave him. Didn't matter what he was. Didn't matter what she was.

Being with him—that was her choice. And she'd been fully aware of the consequences all along.

"How long until you hate this? Me?" His voice was ragged.

Crazy vampire. "Sully, *my* choice." Being a vampire might not have been her lifelong dream, but she knew vamps weren't the heartless killers she'd originally thought. Like humans, like shifters, some were evil.

And some weren't.

The facts were simple to her. She was still breathing. Sully was with her. As for that bastard Corey..."Tell me you killed that murdering shifter."

Sully shook his head, and her heart sank. No, no, he couldn't still be out there. He couldn't—

"Kyle finished him off before I could."

Her shoulders relaxed.

"Seems Corey made a habit of torturing his brother. Kyle left home when he was sixteen and said he'd hoped to never run across his brother again, but then he caught his scent here one night."

He'd killed his brother. Talk about a hard choice. But one that had saved lives. Sadie knew Corey had developed a taste for the kill. She'd seen the horrifying truth in his eyes.

"Corey took Su to send a message to Kyle, didn't he?" she asked.

He nodded. "She was punishment for him. A lure for me."

But they didn't have to worry about Corey any longer. One more killer off the streets.

Pity there were always more out there.

"Can I—can I hold you, love?"

She blinked. Her lips parted in surprise at his halting question. "Of course, Sully. Always. You can—"

He was on the bed before she'd finished speaking. His arms wrapped around her even as his lips took hers. Sully kissed her with a feverish passion and a stark intensity.

Her tongue met his. Her arms locked just as fiercely around him...and deep inside, she heard the purr of her leopard.

Sadie froze. *What? How?*

Sully stiffened against her. "Sadie, no." His words rumbled against her lips. "Don't turn away from me. Things can be the same between us. Give your new life a chance. Give me a chance to—"

Her fingers pushed between them. "I am." His eyes were black. Were hers? Hunger heated her blood, and her teeth had begun to ache.

She wanted to taste him. To bite him. But she could have sworn she'd heard her leopard. *Felt* her.

That was impossible. All the stories said the transformation killed the beast.

And made room for the vampire.

Her fingers caught the V of his shirt. Yanked and sent buttons flying. The white shirt hung loosely on him, now revealing the delicious lines of his muscled chest.

Her mouth was dry. Need filled her. Desperate desire for his body and his blood.

Sadie rose onto her knees. Her mouth pressed against him. Tasted the sweetness of his skin. She tongued his nipple, and the small nub stiffened with the strokes of her tongue.

His hands smoothed down her back. Caught the curves of her bare ass and squeezed.

She bit him. Pierced Sully right above his nipple with her teeth and tasted the wet warmth of his blood.

The leopard purred.

The sound was so familiar to her, but it wasn't a sound she heard with her ears. Only her heart.

As she drank from him, feeling his blood energize her body and send her sensual hunger soaring to a new height, Sadie realized that the stories hadn't been true. Not completely anyway.

"Ah, damn...that feels so...good..." Sully gasped.

Her tongue swiped over the small wound she'd made. Her nipples tightened, and her sex clenched. No wonder vampires were all about blood and sex. It was a freaking great combination.

She lifted her head. His mouth moved to her throat. His teeth scraped over her flesh. "My turn, love..." And he took her. Mouth. Tongue. Teeth.

Sully tumbled her back onto the bed, keeping his teeth on her. *In* her.

Sadie shoved the sheets out of their way. She was naked and more than ready for him.

The bulge of his arousal shoved against the front of his jeans. She unsnapped the button, eased down the zipper with a hiss—and had the hot, heavy length of his cock filling her hands.

Sully's head rose. His face was brutally hard. Etched into taut lines of need. "You almost died on me."

No, correction, she *had* died. That's why she was a vampire now.

"Don't ever do that to me again." Desperation, she knew it when she heard it.

"I won't." Dying wasn't on her agenda. Having mind-blowing sex, yes, that was. Absolutely

The bad guy was dead. She'd survived. And Sully was exactly where she wanted him. Well, *almost.*

He sank into her. A plunging, driving thrust that had her sucking in a sharp breath because he felt so *good.*

She still didn't like things easy, especially not her sex.

Her hips lifted high, then drove right back at him. She needed this—the rush of pleasure, the spike of need. *Needed this. Needed him.*

Because death hadn't held her—no, *he* had. Sully had fought for her and given her a chance to live again. To spend her days and nights with him.

Her muscles tightened as she thundered toward her release. Her sex was so sensitive that every glide and drive of his cock had her twisting beneath him.

His fingers caught her breasts. Fondled her nipples. His cock swelled within her, filling her so fully that she nearly screamed.

He withdrew, thrust deep—

And she did scream. Sadie climaxed on a driving wave of pleasure. Her sex clenched around him, squeezing that thick length tightly, and she gasped as her body shivered with aftershocks of pulsing heat.

Sully was with her. She felt the hot tide of his release within her. Saw the bright flare of pleasure in his eyes.

Oh, yes, he was with her. For every single moment.

He kissed her. She tasted his hunger, his pleasure, his need. And knew that he tasted hers.

A rumble trembled in her throat.

Sully lifted his head. "Sadie?"

Not a rumble, really, more of a purr.

His lips curved into a smile. "I love you, Sadie Townsend."

Her heartbeat had just begun to slow. At his words, the beat immediately kicked up.

"Spend forever with me?" he asked, eyes flickering from black to blue.

Beautiful eyes.

"Try to stop me," she whispered. Forever would be a wonderful start. "I love you, too, Sully." She'd loved him for years.

Loved him.

Mourned him.

Missed him.

Hell, no, he wasn't about to get away from her again. She'd cheated death for her chance with him. Cheated, fought, and won the battle. She was alive, and she had several lifetimes to spend with her Sully. She had—

Forever.

Sadie smiled and kissed him again.

And her leopard was content.

***

Forty-eight hours later, Sadie Townsend stepped into the night with her vampire lover by her side. The stars shimmered so brightly that even the lights of the city couldn't lessen their glow. Music beat in a steady rhythm, coming from the clubs downtown. Voices, whispers, filled her ears, and she drank in the scents from the street.

Her senses were almost as advanced as before. Her strength was still ten times better than a human's.

Sure, the blood hunger would take a bit more adjusting time before she got used to it, but all in all, Sadie thought she was doing pretty well for an undead woman.

Of course, when her brother found out about her new, um, life choice *and* lover choice, Jacob probably wouldn't be thrilled. Serious understatement, she got that.

But he was her brother, and she knew that, no matter what else happened, he loved her. Fangs and blood hunger—he'd learn to deal with them. She knew her brother. He'd rage at first, and then he'd hug her until she felt like he was squeezing her to death.

Brothers. Sometimes they were great. Sometimes they were devils.

Sully's fingers closed around hers. She glanced at him. Sadie couldn't stop the smile that tilted up her lips. Being this happy should be illegal.

She was with Sully. The night was beautiful, and, deep inside, her leopard stretched.

She couldn't shift anymore, but her leopard hadn't died. She was inside, safe, with a strong spirit ready to fight at a moment's notice.

Sully brought her hand to his lips and pressed a kiss against Sadie's palm. She felt the wet swipe of his tongue.

And the surge of her pulse.

Sully could always turn her on. But they had a job to do. As tempted as she was to jump his sexy bones, Owen was waiting to brief them on another case. Always another case.

"Ready to go?" Sully's deep voice stroked over her.

"Yes." No, she wasn't, but the sex would wait.

After all, they had plenty of time.

And, as vampires, plenty of stamina.

"Another night, another city full of killers," he murmured.

Story of their afterlife.

Her fingers tightened around his. "Let's go hunting." Her leopard wanted to play.

She saw the white flash of his teeth as he grinned. Those teeth would be in her neck by morning and she'd love it. *Love it.*

But for now, they had work to do. Owen waited.

And so did the night. Such a beautiful night. Her partner was by her side—a man who would always have her back. He'd fight to the death and beyond for her, she knew it. No more hunting alone, ever.

A perfect team.

The killers they tracked, the monsters gone bad, they wouldn't know what hit them.

Time for the games to begin.

THE END

A NOTE FROM THE AUTHOR

Thank you for reading COME BACK TO ME. I love writing paranormal stories, and it was fun to write a "reunited" tale for Sully and his Sadie. This story was first published in 2010 (back then, it had the title of IN THE DARK and it was released in the BELONG TO THE NIGHT anthology). I was excited to have the chance to bring this tale to you again.

If you'd like to stay updated on my releases and sales, please join my newsletter list.

https://cynthiaeden.com/newsletter/

Again, thank you for reading COME BACK TO ME.

Best,
Cynthia Eden
cynthiaeden.com

ABOUT THE AUTHOR

Cynthia Eden is a *New York Times, USA Today, Digital Book World*, and *IndieReader* best-seller.

Cynthia writes sexy tales of contemporary romance, romantic suspense, and paranormal romance. Since she began writing full-time in 2005, Cynthia has written over one hundred novels and novellas.

Cynthia lives along the Alabama Gulf Coast. She loves romance novels, horror movies, and chocolate.

For More Information

- *cynthiaeden.com*
- *facebook.com/cynthiaedenfanpage*

HER OTHER WORKS

Wilde Ways

- Protecting Piper (Book 1)
- Guarding Gwen (Book 2)
- Before Ben (Book 3)
- The Heart You Break (Book 4)
- Fighting For Her (Book 5)
- Ghost Of A Chance (Book 6)
- Crossing The Line (Book 7)
- Counting On Cole (Book 8)
- Chase After Me (Book 9)
- Say I Do (Book 10)

Dark Sins

- Don't Trust A Killer (Book 1)
- Don't Love A Liar (Book 2)

Lazarus Rising

- Never Let Go (Book One)
- Keep Me Close (Book Two)
- Stay With Me (Book Three)
- Run To Me (Book Four)
- Lie Close To Me (Book Five)
- Hold On Tight (Book Six)

- Lazarus Rising Volume One (Books 1 to 3)
- Lazarus Rising Volume Two (Books 4 to 6)

Dark Obsession Series

- Watch Me (Book 1)
- Want Me (Book 2)
- Need Me (Book 3)
- Beware Of Me (Book 4)
- Only For Me (Books 1 to 4)

Mine Series

- Mine To Take (Book 1)
- Mine To Keep (Book 2)
- Mine To Hold (Book 3)
- Mine To Crave (Book 4)
- Mine To Have (Book 5)
- Mine To Protect (Book 6)
- Mine Box Set Volume 1 (Books 1-3)
- Mine Box Set Volume 2 (Books 4-6)

Bad Things

- The Devil In Disguise (Book 1)
- On The Prowl (Book 2)
- Undead Or Alive (Book 3)
- Broken Angel (Book 4)
- Heart Of Stone (Book 5)
- Tempted By Fate (Book 6)
- Wicked And Wild (Book 7)
- Saint Or Sinner (Book 8)
- Bad Things Volume One (Books 1 to 3)
- Bad Things Volume Two (Books 4 to 6)

- Bad Things Deluxe Box Set (Books 1 to 6)

Bite Series

- Forbidden Bite (Bite Book 1)
- Mating Bite (Bite Book 2)

Blood and Moonlight Series

- Bite The Dust (Book 1)
- Better Off Undead (Book 2)
- Bitter Blood (Book 3)
- Blood and Moonlight (The Complete Series)

Purgatory Series

- The Wolf Within (Book 1)
- Marked By The Vampire (Book 2)
- Charming The Beast (Book 3)
- Deal with the Devil (Book 4)
- The Beasts Inside (Books 1 to 4)

Bound Series

- Bound By Blood (Book 1)
- Bound In Darkness (Book 2)
- Bound In Sin (Book 3)
- Bound By The Night (Book 4)
- Bound in Death (Book 5)
- Forever Bound (Books 1 to 4)

Other Romantic Suspense

- Never Gonna Happen
- One Hot Holiday
- Secret Admirer
- First Taste of Darkness

- Sinful Secrets
- Until Death
- Christmas With A Spy

Manufactured by Amazon.ca
Acheson, AB

13373324R00087